Forget Me Twice

CARINA TAYLOR

Created with Vellum

To power nappers around the world. You truly are amazing. Please teach me your ways.

Synopsis

Have you ever brought your ex-husband home and pretended to still be married?

Yeah, me either.

When my local hospital calls to tell me that my husband has been in an accident, I try to explain the basics to them.

1 I am not married—anymore. (Archie Dunmore is a thing of the past.)

2 If there's a husband in the hospital, it's not mine.

Except Archie is back, and he's been in an accident. One that has left him with amnesia. Yup. He believes we're still happily married. Oh joy.

Too bad for me, the doctor believes it would be best for Archie to remember things on his own. He needs familiar surroundings to heal.

No big shocks.

No emotional trauma.

Which means I can't tell him the truth.

And so I bring my ex-husband home until I can figure out how to ship him safely home to Arizona. (If only my post office allowed live packages...)

Archie bursts back into my life with all the warmth and joy of a freshly married man, confident that I'm the love of his life, and determined to fix the rift between us.

Having a loving husband in my house is getting awkward. Especially when Archie is desperately trying to remember what I've worked so hard to forget.

How do I tell him that he walked out on me?

What's a girl to do with an amnesiac ex-husband at her breakfast table?

Prologue

MARGARET: THE OVERLY HELPFUL, SELF-APPOINTED MATCHMAKER IN OUR STORY

Eighty-seven is full of surprises. For instance, whoever said we should 'age with grace' obviously never experienced rheumatoid arthritis.

Whoever said you couldn't enjoy life at eighty-seven had also been dead wrong.

I stir my coffee with my silver spoon.

At eighty-seven you no longer save your fine china for special occasions. You discover that every day is special for a reason.

At this age I've come to appreciate the most important things in life. A strong cup of coffee, some juicy gossip, and loved ones nearby. My loved ones go beyond my immediate family and extend to many of the people living in Green Valley, a town I've lived in for sixty-five years. I didn't know that my family would expand to include an entire town. That I would have so many 'children' to worry over.

I've been happily teaching piano to multiple generations of children, hosting game nights and generally helping out anywhere in town that I can. I did recently have to step down as mayor because my doctor assured me it was doing nothing good for my blood pressure.

Today is a slow day for me. It's my cleaning day.

I hate cleaning days.

A low rumble shakes the house. My wine glass collection rattles.

It's probably another plane. They're always flying in way too low over my neighborhood.

The rumbling grows louder. With a huff, I stand and make my way to the sliding glass door.

Sure enough. There's a plane. It's coming in low. Fast. Looks as though it's going to take the tops off the houses even.

"I keep telling them that the planes fly too low here." I mumble. But they've never flown *this* low. Something flies off the back of the plane. It looks like a piece of fabric—though my eyes could be playing tricks on me.

"It looks like they're going to crash," I comment to my dust bunnies that are not being swept up like they should be. I really should be trying one of those robot vacuums that Bailey was telling me about.

My phone is ringing in my pocket. *Think of the devil.* I answer it as the plane stutters. "Bailey."

Bailey is a child I've known for years. She's also my neighbor and the mother of three now. We have wine Wednesdays together. She pretends like she's checking on the elderly neighbor and it gets her out of the house and gives her a break from the kids. I make sure to call and complain about some imaginary ailment so she keeps having an excuse to come over. It's become a nice routine of ours.

"Are you watching this?" She asks breathlessly.

"Yes," I answer quickly as the plane splutters. We've complained to each other enough about the planes that I know she hates the loud engines because it wakes up her napping toddler.

Then Bailey mutters a word under her breath I'm pretty sure she wouldn't want her kids to hear if they were in the same room. And then I repeat the word. The plane is swooping down directly in front of Bailey's house, barely missing the roof.

"He's crashing!" I announce. Good thing I'm not teaching any piano lessons this morning. I might traumatize someone.

The plane is definitely crashing. No 'maybe' about it.

A wing clips the edge of a gutter. The plane drifts over the top of a trampoline, then the engine cuts out completely before it collapses accordion style into my yard.

"Margaret!" Bailey is shrieking in my ear. "Margaret! Answer me! Are you okay?"

"I'm fine," I reply as I unlock the glass door and slide it open. The plane is smoking slightly and there is going to be one hell of a lawn care bill to fix the damage it's done.

"I'm going to hang up and call nine-one-one," Bailey says.

"Good idea, dear. Call me back after you do."

"I'll do you one better. I'll come over there in person. Don't go near that wreck! I don't want you hurt."

And then she's gone. It always makes me laugh when young people tell you not to do something. As if we somehow accidentally survived this long without them.

A door swings open from the plane and a bloodied man falls to the ground. He lands on his hands and knees then looks up at me.

I'd know that face anywhere.

Archie Dunmore's come home.

I always knew this day would come. Too much unfinished business.

But looking at him now?

Boy, oh boy do I have my work cut out for me.

Chapter One
MEYER

"I'm sorry to tell you this, but your husband has been in an accident," an unfamiliar voice tells me.

The words drift through the phone, ringing in my ears.

"I think I misheard you," I say as I shut my front door with a sharp slam—it never latches correctly unless I do.

Hanging my purse on the hook above my entryway table, I turn and stare at myself in the mirror. My bangs are not where they should be, and my hands feel empty after delivering my packages to the post office, where the postal worker pretends like she hasn't seen me before.

I see Janice, the mail clerk, every Tuesday and Friday when I ship my orders. We like to play the *Oh, who are you?* and *Can I interest you in a book of stamps?* game.

No, Janice, you can't interest me, not since the price of stamps went up a penny. I can't afford that habit.

"Your husband was involved in an accident," the voice repeats, reminding me that I answered the call to a number I didn't recognize. Sometimes, I like to live dangerously. "Ma'am, your husband has been injured."

Vocabulary wasn't my strong suit in grade school, but I have a firm enough grasp on it now to realize that an accident usually results in an injury.

There is one slight problem with her explanation, however.

"I'm not married."

There's a painful silence as I kick off my shoes and stretch my toes, waiting for the telemarketer's pitch. It's probably a life-insurance scam. I bend down and slide my shoes onto my shoe shelf.

"You are Meyer Dunmore, aren't you?" Her voice takes on an exasperated tone.

Yes, I think I know my name, thank you very much.

These scam callers are getting good. She asked if I was Meyer Dunmore when I first answered the phone. I now regret saying yes.

"Yes." I draw out the word into a quiet hiss as I wait for her to explain. I need my daily power nap. And now, I'm missing it because of a spam call.

"Archie Dunmore was brought into the emergency room today at Green Valley General. Unfortunately, he was involved in a minor accident, and I'm afraid some complications would be better explained in person."

Archie Dunmore.

My heart drops to my socked feet. "Accident?" My voice tremors even though I do my best to focus on the words I'm hearing.

"Yes. He's been injured. That's why I'm calling you."

"I'm sorry. I don't understand. It's just that...Archie Dunmore is my ex-husband. That's why I'm confused."

Archie Dunmore had once filled a piece of my soul that I hadn't known was missing, then crushed it entirely when he walked out of my life a year ago.

"Well, you're listed as his only emergency contact. And it says you're his wife." She states it in a way that says that the paperwork couldn't possibly be wrong.

Well, it can be, Karen.

"There's no one else listed? Our last names are the same because I haven't taken the time to switch mine back yet. You probably meant to reach Holly Dunmore. That's his mother. How bad is it? Where is he?" I ask, though I know that when he left me, he fled to his home state of Arizona. I tell her as much. "I'm not even in the same state. I'm in Oregon."

"He is, too. I already said Green Valley General." A heavy sigh deafens my ear.

I'm a burden to this woman, and she wants me to know it. But why can't she just explain what's going on?

"So, Archie has been hurt? In an accident?" These words are familiar, almost as if someone just said them.

"Yes...I'm afraid he's suffering a—" She stops herself and then repeats her earlier pronouncement, "Well, he's been in an accident."

Suffering. It's more information than I had three seconds ago, but I'm still not sure what she wants me to do about it. Physical or emotional suffering? I need her to elaborate. Despite leaving me, despite being my ex, I need him to be okay.

"But he's going to be all right?"

"We'll be able to give you more information in person. We prefer to disclose news face to face," she answers.

"Did he stub a toe or lose a leg?" I pry.

"It would be best if you spoke with the doctor." Now, she sounds tired. Maybe she needs a nap, too.

"A bathroom accident or a car accident?"

"Please drive carefully." She doesn't sound like she means it.

With that, the pesky woman hangs up, and I'm left imagining Archie lying in a casket. He's made me mad in the past—furious, even—but I would never wish an accident on him.

Despite the nurse's reminder to drive carefully, I drive like I'm auditioning for a demolition derby. I leave muddy tracks in my yard, screech onto the road in front of a minivan, then blow through every stoplight in town—all three of them.

I park in the front-row spot at the hospital that says *Patient Offloading*, then dart inside and head straight for the ER waiting room.

"Hi. I'm here for Archie Dunmore."

The powerful smell of antiseptic fills my nostrils as I wait for the receptionist to respond. She taps her thumb against the phone and speaks a few more words before hanging up and answering me.

"We don't allow visitors in the ER."

"You. Called. Me." And I will happily walk out right now if she doesn't escort me back, because I would bet my last dollar that Archie doesn't know I'm still listed as his emergency contact on his medical information.

She glances up. "You said Archie Dunmore. Are you the emergency contact?"

"It seems so," I say between clenched teeth. The anxiousness welling up in my soul at the thought of seeing the man I once considered to be my soul mate has me barely managing social niceties.

"All right, I'll buzz you through. Head to the triage desk, and the nurse will direct you."

I stand in front of the double doors and wait for the telltale buzz. The doors swing open automatically, and I wonder if this is how Lucy felt when she first stepped into the wardrobe.

Then, I move forward. My backpack purse bangs against me with each step.

I haven't seen Archie in a year. The last fight we had was oh-so impressive. The divorce was uncontested and required neither of us to be present. Yet, I have to see him for myself. I need to know that he will be okay after this accident. Then, I can go home. I'll take that power nap that didn't happen.

The triage nurse is more helpful than Friendly Fran at the front desk. This one points me directly to Archie's room and tells me she's glad I made it.

Taking a shaky, sterile-air-filled breath, I rap my knuckles on the large wooden door and push it open slowly. I brace myself for the sight.

Archie lies on a hospital bed. His long body is bent awkwardly, as though he is trying to find a comfortable way to rest. There's a bandage on his head, wrapped on top of his thick, medium-length hair. It seems darker than

I remember. The cut on his cheekbone gives him a dangerous air, taking away from his usual boyish charm.

Is that a five-o'clock shadow I see?

He's wearing a crisp white shirt, splattered with blood. A suit jacket and tie are folded on a seat next to him. The only time Archie would be caught in a hospital gown was if he was dead. So, he must not be too injured if he was able to refuse one.

A couple of nicks stand out on his chin. He's been hurt, but still, he's here. In the flesh.

I want to hug him. ~~I want his love.~~ I want a reckoning.

But I probably won't get any of those things.

What will he say? Will this be a practical transaction? Does he need my help to get home? Maybe he wants me to hand over his favorite Christmas socks that I kept after the divorce. He might still want his ratty, old sweatshirt back.

I can tell the moment he senses he's not alone. His body tenses, and then he opens his eyes and turns to face me.

Instead of the curt, hurtful, or brusque meeting I expect this to be, his voice is warm and joyful as he greets me. It reminds me of the first year we were married.

"Meyer!" Archie's face breaks into a relieved smile. A cheerful smile.

That can't be right. Maybe it's the painkillers working, because when he left me a year ago, it was not on speaking terms.

"Archie..." I draw out his name, wanting to call him Archibald as all the pain of that last fight comes crashing into me, battling the memories of other happier times.

"They said I could go home as soon as you got here," he says as he reaches a hand out for me. It shakes almost imperceptibly, and there are cuts on his knuckles.

I sigh, reminding myself that this man was in an accident. He's grateful to be alive, and he needs someone there with him. And apparently, I'm his ticket out of here, so maybe that's why he's relieved to see me.

I place my hand in his. Those calluses are so familiar yet so foreign. I know the sensation of those hands—everywhere. Yet, it's been so long since I've touched them. Since they've touched me.

This is very normal—mundane, even—I snap at myself. He's in shock, and it's only right I offer him comfort.

"It's okay, Archie. I'll make sure you get home as soon as possible," I say soothingly, because it seems right in this situation.

"Thanks, Meyer. What would I do without you?"

I'm pretty sure I hear a record scratch somewhere. What would he do without me? He's been *doing* without me for an entire year now.

He frowns and flinches as he studies my face. "What's wrong?"

"Where to start?" I mutter.

He reaches up and touches the bandage on his forehead. "I'm sorry. I'm a little out of it right now, but they promised me it looked worse than it is."

I decide not to comment on that.

The door swings open, and a doctor bustles in—and not the doctor who stitched up my nephew Elijah's chin after he cracked it at the local community pool. This doctor looks fresh out of medical school and would have patients swooning for his attention in no time.

Well, hello, hello.

I glance down at Archie, who's now frowning and glancing between the two of us. The doctor introduces himself as Dr. Tripp Sharpe.

Archie's earlier smile is gone, and now, he's busy trying to sit up and look less injured than he really is.

"Stop fussing," I hiss at him as he jerks at the IV cords.

If he's not careful, he'll yank them out.

Dr. Sharpe ignores our interaction and reviews the charts. "Looks like your scans came back with some minor swelling and bruising, but with lots of rest and sleep, you'll be back to yourself in no time."

"Thank you, Dr. Sharpe." I cannot look at Archie because he seems to be scooting closer to me.

He still holds my hand in his, and it's sending a confusing signal to my brain.

I need to get out of here before I say or do something I'll regret, so I proactively direct the conversation. "When can we send Archie home? I'm sure we're all ready for that." And I do mean *all*.

"Could I have a word with you out in the hall?" Dr. Sharpe asks me as he glances back and forth between Archie and me in the classic *I-have-something-to-tell-you* way that people think is so sly. It isn't. The whole world sees and recognizes that look, but they take pity on the one who is casting it and pretend not to notice.

Archie frowns as he watches the look pass between the doctor and me.

Hopefully, Archie won't question it too much. His fingers squeeze mine gently, but then his other hand lands on my hip—halfway on my ass. His large hands are very memorable.

My back stretches tight, and I look at the doctor in a panic, as if he can explain why my ex-husband is being so possessive.

I don't bother saying anything to Archie because I don't want to fight—not right now.

"Should we go talk now?" My voice is panicky because I'd love nothing more than to step into the hall and clear my head while I learn what the hell is going on.

I pull my hand from Archie's, and I don't like that I miss the sensation of it in mine.

"What do you need to talk about in the hall?" Archie's voice has a bite in it.

Dr. Sharpe doesn't look at me, but instead addresses Archie. "I need to discuss aftercare with her. Make sure she can fill your prescriptions for you. You need to rest that head of yours. And no driving. Or flying."

Archie still looks suspicious—and it's a look I know well.

Given the fact that he has a bump on his head, I decide to pretend like he has the right to that look. That the hand on my ass is out of habit. For now. Until I can ship him back to where he came from.

"Wait, what do you mean *flying*?" The words finally register as I glance between Archie and the doctor.

Archie seems to find the ceiling very interesting for someone with such a guilty face.

"His accident was a plane crash," Dr. Sharpe

explains in a monotone voice, as though he heals a plane-crash victim every day.

I don't take my eyes off Archie. I told him he would get hurt from flying planes. I *told* him I didn't want to be the one picking up the pieces. He flung it in my face in that last nasty fight. And now, he expects me to pretend like everything is completely fine and that it's a normal thing to help my ex-husband out of the hospital.

It couldn't have been something mundane, like a fender bender. Or him backing into the mailbox. Possibly even skinning his knee while rollerblading. Nope. Not my ex-husband. Because if Archie Dunmore were to get in an accident, it *would* be a plane crash. He doesn't like to be average. He always likes to go above and beyond the mark. Nothing expected from him.

Archie finally looks at me. "I'm sorry, Meyer. You were right. I got lost in the clouds and ended up here."

Anyone else, and I would have taken them literally. But with Archie, I know he's talking about getting lost in his thoughts. He probably got distracted and flew straight into a tree or some type of nonsense like that.

I nod once. "I'll speak with the doctor, and then you can be on your way home."

The remorse on his face tugs at my heartstrings.

He's disoriented from the wreck, and that's why I'm sympathetic toward him, I remind myself.

Once he's back on his feet, the walls will be back up, and we won't speak again.

Dr. Sharpe leads the way out of the room, and I have a hard time pulling my eyes away from Archie. His dark hair falls forward and to the side in an effortless swoosh.

The door closes, shutting off my inventory of Archie, and Dr. Sharpe jumps straight into the diagnosis.

"He has post-traumatic amnesia—PTA."

"He what?" I slam my hand against the wall to catch myself. I accidentally punch the hand sanitizer perched there, and a pink foam shoots out onto my wrist. "Amnesia?" I repeat as I rub the hand sanitizer into my hands. Can never be too careful, especially in a hospital.

Dr. Sharpe's eyes focus on my wrist, and he clears his throat. "I'm afraid he thinks it's April."

The purple pages of my planner come to mind. "That is bad. It's almost June."

"Of two years ago," he adds.

Somewhere in the dark recesses of my mind, I realize that Dr. Sharpe is staring at me.

I stare back. Two years. *Amnesia.*

That's when someone forgets things. Important things. Whole blocks of time. Sometimes certain people. There has to be a solution. This is the part where he'll tell me the man needs brain surgery. That would be the next logical step.

"How long will the operation last?"

"Operation?" Dr. Sharpe furrows his brows, and I realize that *furrow* is a strange way to think of eyebrows.

Why do we call it furrowed brows?

"To fix the amnesia?"

He smiles slightly, and I can't tell if it's a sympathetic smile or if he's trying to hold back a laugh at my expense.

"The only thing that can heal amnesia is time," he explains slowly.

I blow a breath out through my lips. "So, why am I

here exactly?"

"You're his emergency contact," Dr. Sharpe says. "And his wife."

"Ex," I blurt out. "Does no one in this hospital realize that I can't help him?"

"He seems to think you can." The condoling look on his face makes me want to cry. "He's lost whole chunks of time. But he knows you. He says he remembers marrying you. He remembers your home address. But you say you're divorced. When was that?"

"Last May," I reply around the lump in my throat. "A full year."

On one hand, I can see how this is problematic for the doctor, but I want him to know that thing lying on the bed in the room next to us is not coming home with me.

"Oh dear," he says as he glances through his charts.

I stare at the young doctor.

Oh dear—that seems to be such a mild expression for my mood and definitely not the word I would have used.

If Archie thinks it's April of two years ago, then he thinks we're still married.

He thinks I'm his wife.

Even worse, he thinks we're *happily* married.

He doesn't know about the big fight we had or the million little moments that had led up to it. He doesn't know that he chose to walk away from me...

My heart wrenches and soars at the same time. *Archie doesn't know.*

For one brief moment, I get a horrible—and possibly brilliant—idea. Bring him home. Pretend we're still married. Live our lives together like we always wanted to.

Reality crashes my brainstorm before it has too long to flood my soul and take root. "He thinks we're still married? Why don't I tell him the truth?"

Dr. Sharpe holds out a hand toward me, placating me. He's careful to not touch me, simply stretching out his hand. It looks like a strange floating apparition extending from his oversized scrubs.

"I'm not saying you couldn't...but his mind is in a fragile state. It's generally best to let it heal on its own. It will be harder for it to heal when it has emotional stress. He needs some time—that's all. He already understands that he has amnesia and doesn't remember everything. So, maybe you could help him until someone else can take him off your hands. I understand your dilemma, but truly, the best thing for him is to be in a familiar environment and given the chance to heal. And right now, you are that familiar environment."

"Does this mean I'm going to have to take care of all of his physical needs?"

Showering. Naked. So very naked. And I can picture it clear as day.

That suspicious smile is back on the doctor's face, and I purge my thoughts in case he can read them.

"Not unless you want to. He's physically sound. It's his mind that needs time to heal."

I let out a breath of relief. I will not have to carry Archie to the bathroom. But that still leaves a big dilemma.

I had promised in sickness and in health, and he walked away in health.

Chapter Two

I'm bringing my ex-husband home with me.

There's no other solution. The hospital policy doesn't allow him to stay in the emergency room indefinitely, even though that would have been my preference. They could keep him, raise him to be a functioning adult.

Dr. Sharpe tells me he'll have the triage nurse get everything ready for Archie's discharge.

Then, he leaves me to face the inevitable.

I stare at the door to Archie's room for the second time in a day.

Two years. He's forgotten seven hundred thirty–plus days. Two years is a big gap. Even worse, that was before we hit our rough patch. We hadn't started fighting yet. Archie believes we're blissfully, happily together still.

Check him out, send him home. Easy-peasy. I'm sure his mom can get him by the end of the day. Phoenix isn't *that* far. A twenty hour drive or a three hour flight: either one could be accomplished in a twenty-four hour period.

I crack open the door and stare through the two-inch

space. Archie's still lying in bed. He hasn't magically gone home.

I'm halfway waiting for a reality-show crew to show up and tell me it's an epic prank they all planned.

But Archie senses the open door, and his eyes lock onto my one eye that's looking through the narrow opening.

"Meyer, come in! I've been dying to know what the doctor said." He chuckles at his own word use. "Well, hopefully not dying."

I open the door wide enough to stick my head through, but I still don't enter the room. "You have amnesia. Okay, bye."

I pull back and close the door. To my surprise, an uproarious laugh comes from the other side of the door.

I open the door and slip inside this time, pressing my back against it as it closes with a click.

Archie is still laughing as he looks at me. "Stop it. It hurts to laugh," he gasps.

"I'm not joking, Archie. That's what the doctor said."

He finally gets control of his laughter. He holds a hand against his shoulder as he sits up. "Meyer, you don't have to worry. The doctor already explained that to me. He *tried* to explain everything to me, anyway. I have to admit, it's strange to wake up and have someone tell me I've lived two years of life that I don't even remember a tiny bit. But I'm glad to see you're still you." He smiles slowly at that. "You still don't want to deliver bad news."

I jerk my shoulders back and squelch down a childish retort. I want to snap back that I can deliver bad news better than anyone else, but obviously not, because I don't want to be standing here in the same room with him when he does remember the last two years.

A brisk knock has me jumping away from the door before the triage nurse bursts in with a folder of papers.

The nurse greets Archie with a cheery smile. "Well, hello there! Sounds like you'll be going home sooner rather than later."

I'd like to choose the later option, please.

Archie grins as he begins signing wherever she points. He never did bother reading things he signed. Said it was a waste of his time and energy. Said if someone ever bothered to actually scam him, then it would be kudos to them.

I shake my head as I listen to the nurse prattle off about prescription-strength acetaminophen.

Archie glances over the nurse's shoulder at me and winks.

My phone chimes at that precise moment, giving me a great reason to ignore that wink.

I unlock the screen and stare at the text message. It's from my PR manager who I hired to help market my business. She's incredibly hands-on with a heavy dose of intensity, but she's been marvelous for my business, and I think we're sort of friends now.

Willa: I have big news! HUGE.

Probably not as big as mine.

I scroll through my texts and find another one from my sister, Bailey.

Bailey: Did you know there was a plane wreck in town???

I text Bailey back.

Me: Oh, really?

If I tell her I'm standing next to the plane-wreck victim and who the plane-wreck victim is, she'll be here in a heartbeat. I need some time to figure out what I'm going to do about this situation without an overprotective older sister.

"Oh, I forgot the other folder! I'll be right back." The nurse leaves the room as quickly as she entered it, and I'm left there alone with Archie.

I need to call Holly. That would be the proper order of business.

"It's going to be okay, Meyer," he tells me as he holds out a hand to me. "My memory is going to come back, and it will be as though nothing has changed."

That's what I'm afraid of.

I'd made it through the rage stage of divorce. I'd even made it through the missing-him stage of divorce. I'm now in the try-to-be-happy stage, and I'm scared to death that I'll always be missing a piece of my heart to Archie.

The rest of the release process is painfully quick. A few more forms signed, a book-sized release form.

They don't even offer to keep him overnight or until he is healed. They don't send a qualified nurse home with us either.

The best I get is a business card from Dr. Sharpe.

Even though he went a step above what was required by writing his cell phone number on the back, I'm woefully unprepared to take care of my patient.

I thank the doctor for the cell number—not the usual

protocol of an ER doctor, but then again, an amnesia case probably isn't incredibly common.

"Of course," Dr. Sharpe says as he smiles at both of us. "I wish you the best of luck. Call if you have any questions."

Then, he's hurrying off to another room at a jog. Another life to save.

"I can't decide if I want to be his best friend or if I can't stand him," Archie says thoughtfully beside me.

I study his face while he's preoccupied watching the doctor run away. Archie's face still has the sharp angles. The strong jaw. His beat-up remnants of a suit attest to his corporate job in Phoenix—the 'more fulfilling dream' he pursued.

I wonder what he would do if I ripped the shirt off him and shook it in front of his face, maybe ask him, *Where did this land you?*

But that would be too tongue-in-cheek, even for me, so instead, I nod and say, "I'm sure Dr. Sharpe would be a nice friend, but you can worry about that later. Let's go."

Archie is looking a little haggard as we walk through the main lobby to the double sliding-glass doors. I slow my walk so he can keep up.

"Here, let me carry that." I take the plastic bag from him that's carrying his phone, wallet, keys, and a torn suit jacket.

He hands it over and picks up his pace. He reaches for my hand, and I pretend like I don't notice as I dodge out of the sliding doors.

"I parked in the front."

I march through the covered offloading zone to my

car, Archie following behind me more slowly again. If I walk in front of him, then I don't have to look at him. And I can pretend like it's completely normal to go pick up your ex-husband from the hospital and bring him home.

It's fine. Completely fine. Everything's normal.

My name is in the dictionary under *normal*. I'm the synonym. Archie is my antonym.

I look at the parking space where I left my car. There's a security guard standing there with his hands on his hips, staring at it. This can't be good. Can security guards give tickets? I don't know.

"Did you know that this is an offloading zone only?" he asks in a grating tone.

I look at the sign that clearly says *Patient Offloading*.

After studying the sign for far too long, I hear Archie clear his throat. If I turn around and see him smiling, I don't know if I can control myself. There might be a Hulk tendency deep in my soul if I find him laughing at me. I don't turn around.

"Thought it said *on*loading. I'm sorry. I was in such a hurry when the hospital called and said he was in an accident." I jerk a thumb over my shoulder to the giant problem in question.

Archie hums his agreement.

Don't turn around, Meyer, I remind myself as the security guard looks at me like I've lost my mind. And I'm about to agree with him.

"You know, if you glance at that sign quickly, it looks like it says *onloading* rather than *offloading*," Archie chimes in.

The security guard glances at the sign. He stares at it.

Soon, he's swinging his head back and forth slowly. And then he shakes his head quickly.

Then, he turns to face me. "He's right. It does look like it says *onloading* at a quick glance." The guard nods his head once, then points to the car. "Hurry up and get it out of here."

I unlock the car and point Archie toward the passenger seat because he looks like he wants to jump into the driver's seat. That would have been a laugh. A big, deep, belly laugh.

"Listen, you hit your head hard enough to not remember a couple of years." I pat the roof of the car as I stare him down. "If you think I'm going to let you behind the wheel of this car..." I trail off, letting him fill in the blank for himself.

"You won't sleep with me for a week?"

"No!" And I mean that on so many levels.

How could he even be thinking of that at a time like this?

"Oh, good. I'd hate to have that hanging over my head."

He winks and climbs into the passenger seat, and I'm left standing there, wondering at what point I used sex as a weapon. *Did I?*

Wait, I am not going to stand in the hospital parking lot and debate my marital faults while my ex-husband sits in the car with amnesia.

Shaking my head, I climb in behind the wheel. His presence makes my car seem much smaller. Archie isn't huge. It's not like I barely reach his belly button, like a tragic heroine in a story. No. He has the decency to be a matchable size to my five-eight, standing at five-ten himself. He always claims to be six feet tall, but I've seen his height on his medical charts and know that he's not six feet.

My car is spacious. There's plenty of room in the front. There's even a roomy backseat. But now? With him in here? I might as well be driving him home on the back of a moped. Possibly a tricycle.

It's silent in the car as I adjust my seat and mirrors for an inordinately long time.

"I'm sorry," he says. "I know you've been worried about me flying."

I offer him a tight smile as I pull out of the hospital parking lot. "Let's not talk about this right now. You probably need some quiet for a little bit to let your mind rest."

Archie nods. "You're right about that." He leans back against the headrest. "I'm going to close my eyes for a minute. This headache is out of this world."

"Good idea."

With that, we lapse into an awkward silence, but at least it's quiet.

Women everywhere have interacted with their ex-husbands. Some of them have even brought their ex-husbands to their house. So many of them. I'm in a class of women who could fill—I don't know—some big place.

I'm sure many women have brought back a husband who has amnesia. It's very common. In fact, I should think about starting a support group. We could meet weekly and talk about the struggles and joys of bringing back an ex-husband who remembers you more fondly than you do him.

Weekly meetings seem like a bit too much. Maybe once a month? No, still too people-ish.

An online forum. I have to start an online forum. That is the answer. I'll find all the other women who are in my exact same situation, and we could support each other through our strange and *completely* normal lives.

"The doctor told me that I crashed in a neighborhood," Archie pipes up. "I'd like to look before we go home. I need to see. Maybe if I see it, I'll remember." He reaches a hand across the console and pats my hand, as though he's going to reassure me.

Jumping, I bump my elbow against the door. I manage to keep my eyes on the road because if I don't, I'll drive us into the steep ditch.

"Which neighborhood?" I ask.

Archie turns on the radio, tuning in to a local news station.

Maybe I should have asked Bailey how she knew about the plane crash. It couldn't have possibly been on the news yet.

"Did you hurt anyone else?"

He shakes his head. "I don't think so. I think the doctor would've said if I had. But I think it was a big deal. I'd like to see exactly what happened. I was a little out of it when I crawled from the plane."

I turn down the radio because there's too much noise and I'll forget how to drive. "Do you remember exactly where they said you crashed?"

This time, I do risk a glance at him. He has a guilty look on his face, which I hope that anyone who crashed an airplane would have. I appreciate his appropriate mood.

"Margaret's house," he finally says.

Something similar to a wheeze makes its way out of me.

"No."

He nods. "Yes. I'm afraid it's that bad."

I understand why he needs to drive by and take a look now.

Margaret Eventhall is well-liked in our community. She's well-liked by me and Archie. She's a wonderful woman. She's also a retired woman, who has time to make phone calls, texts, and even TikToks.

What she knows, the entire town knows. It also explains how Bailey knows. Bailey lives in the same neighborhood as Margaret and most likely witnessed the fiery event.

Which means, I was probably the last to know that Archie Dunmore was back in town.

Which *also* means, I need to have a little phone call with Bailey and explain the situation. Hard to do when I'm sitting *next* to the situation.

I turn left on Walnut and slow down as we approach a gray house with a backyard—and an airplane sitting in said backyard.

It's the Cirrus SR20. I know it because it's the plane he talked about buying forever. And I heard—through expert social-media stalking—that he had bought one.

I slow down as I study the wreckage. I hope that Archie doesn't expect civil conversation right now. Because I'm mad. Is he my ex-husband? Yes. Do I have any business telling him what he can and cannot do? Again, yes, when it comes to his life. I told him over and over again that his interest in flying was going to get him killed.

"Hell, would you look at that?" Archie murmurs to himself.

It's a miracle he's alive. The airplane took apart the entire fence between Margaret's and her neighbor's houses. The fence that separates their backyards from one another is no longer standing. The tree in the corner is leaning precariously, looking as though it were the final brake for the plane.

The front of the airplane is completely smashed in. Glass is broken, and it looks as though someone tried to play the plane like an accordion.

I stop the car in the middle of the street since there's no other traffic in sight.

Archie stares at it as he rolls down the window. "I wish I could remember what happened. The chute should have deployed, but I don't see it."

The tail is barely hanging on.

A soft wind picks up, blowing the metal slat back and forth. I can hear it creaking outside the car.

Archie frowns as he studies the wreckage. "I wonder what I was doing. I want to know how that wreck happened."

"Me too," I agree. I'd really like to know what he was doing, too.

He hadn't been back to Green Lake in a year. What was he doing here now?

"Margaret's house looks different," he says slowly.

My phone chimes, but I ignore it. "She painted. And an ice storm killed the big tree in the front yard."

"She was home when I crashed, I think. The doctor said that she was the first one to help me. She's probably told everyone already."

"My thoughts as well," I reply.

He chuckles. "Should we stop in and say hi? Let her know I'm alive? No doubt, she's already planned the funeral. The playlist is probably already decided."

A laugh bubbles up as he voices exactly what I was thinking. But I can't let him near Margaret. She'll spill everything, the truth will traumatize him, and then he'll never heal, and I'll be stuck with a husband who doesn't remember that I'm mad at him for divorcing me.

"Let's get back to the house. That's the most important thing right now. You need rest. The doctor said lots of sleep is what's going to heal you the fastest."

"You're kidding." He has the balls to look shocked, as if I suggested he snort a line of cocaine to heal his mind.

Archie hates sleep. It's a necessary evil in his mind. It wastes precious time that he could spend doing something else. *Anything else.*

"Archie, you're going to get as much sleep as possible. And if I have to lock you in a room, then I will."

He waggles his eyebrows. "Only as long as you're in bed with me."

"Nope. Your head does not need to be jostled or bumped any more than it already has been."

He reaches over and rests a hand on my thigh, squeezing lightly. My whole body seizes up. He's sent an electrical shock throughout my body.

"We could be gentle..."

Some things haven't changed over time, and my body's dynamic reaction to his touch is one of them. My mind battles against itself as I wonder if I should slap his hand or hold it. In the past, it was routine for him to rest a hand on my thigh. It didn't matter who was driving. If we were in the car together, he had his hand on me.

I reach down and pat his hand twice, then pry his fingers off of me, placing his hand back in his lap as I turn onto my road. "I don't want you getting any ideas. We're going to be focused on your recovery—and only your recovery," I add sternly.

His fingers drum against his leg, as though he's debating sending his hand back over.

"No," I say. "Archie, I'm serious. You were in a plane wreck, for goodness' sake. You need to heal."

"What about a massage to make me feel better?" The hopeful tone in his voice is not innocent.

"No." This time, it comes out a little waspish.

"What about a massage to make *you* feel better?"

I huff. "Why would I need a massage?"

"Because you seem very uptight right now, and honestly, it makes me so happy that you care so much for me. That you're so grumpy that I almost died."

I turn slowly to look at him in disbelief. If he wants a near-death experience, I could happily give him one right now. Instead, I shake my head and focus on getting us home—safely.

Heal him. Keep him out of my pants. Don't let him break my heart again.

Easy-peasy.

Chapter Three

I park the car in my driveway because there's no room in my small garage. I'm in the middle of reorganizing my storage system so that shipping items is more seamless—one of the main reasons I'm considering selling this house. But my attachment to this place runs a lot deeper than I realized.

We purchased this small three bed, one bath cottage on a huge lot with the intention of raising a family here. Archie and I even had a special 'expand the house' fund for when we could finally afford to add on. But it had been perfect for us as a starter home. And although it's a little tight running a business out of it, it's not impossible. My love for the home surpasses my need for space.

I shut the car off, refusing to turn my head and look at Archie. It's too strange. I wonder what will catch his notice. What he'll remember and what will seem new to him.

"We painted!" His words are bewildered.

I slowly turn my head a fraction of an inch. I see his wide eyes taking in every detail of the house in the yard.

We didn't paint. *I* did. He was gone already by the time I picked one of the four thousand three hundred sixty-eight paint options. But I don't say that. I only smile and nod.

"The azalea bush is gone," he says with wonder.

I take a slow, steady breath and remind myself that he doesn't know what a colossal ass he's been this year. As far as he remembers, he's still present, doting Archie.

"Yes, just a few improvements."

He smiles and nods. "I'm still so glad we bought this little house. Aren't you?"

I think about the fact that I snapped a few pictures last week while debating about listing it. I've toyed with the idea for six months now, battling with myself over the fact that I love this house, but there are too many memories lingering here for me to be at peace in my own home. So many memories of Archie.

I need a different house. Maybe a different continent, at this rate. Something to help me get over Archie. But instead, I'm preparing to make up the guest bed for him.

Climbing out of the car, I'm greeted by Gatsby. He's a giant orange cat with a questionable attitude.

He rubs against my legs, leaving a trail of hair against my black yoga pants. The traitor turns to Archie.

He even has the gall to mosey over and greet him, too.

My mind screams at him, *He left us, Gatsby! He doesn't deserve your love!*

But I put a lid on the raging storm inside me and, instead, walk up the sidewalk to unlock the door. I hear

Archie talking to Gatsby and acting as though he never abandoned us. I swing open the door and step inside. Archie follows me, carrying Gatsby, who shall now remain nameless.

Gatsby has full rein of both the house and the outdoors. I'm always worried that he'll be run over one day, but he enjoys the freedom afforded him in the outdoors. The one time I tried to keep him completely pent-up inside, he became so lethargic that I rushed him to the twenty-four-hour vet. Turns out, cats can get depressed, too. I allowed him outside again, and he's been perfectly happy ever since.

"Why am I so tired?" Archie asks as he strokes the cat's head, still taking in every detail of the house.

It's still the same small bungalow it has always been, except a few minor decor changes. A three bed, one bath with hardly any storage space. Minimalism has been forced upon us by a lack of square footage.

I stare at him, wondering if he's joking or not. But he looks serious. I wasn't sure how much he'd changed over the last year, but now, I know that he is as indomitable as ever, not believing he could possibly be subject to human feelings such as exhaustion.

"You were in a plane crash. And you broke your head. You probably have bruises all over. You have stitches where the glass cut you. Should I go on?"

"Details." He smiles at me and reaches out to squeeze my hand, still holding Gatsby in his other arm. "I'm sure I'll be back to normal tomorrow," he says.

"We can only hope," I mutter.

Our hands are now linked together by a strong electric current. He looks perfectly relieved while I'm busy battling a tornado inside my chest. I stare at him, not sure what to do about the hand surrounding mine.

He keeps touching me.

My raging protective conscience is screaming at me, *Shields up!*

But another part of my brain hurries to Archie's defense.

He doesn't know, I tell myself so I don't jerk my hand out of his.

I watch the light in his eyes dim a little as my hand remains limp in his. It's the second time I've resisted his physical affection. I have to remind myself that he doesn't know that we're divorced. So, I force a smile on my face.

"Come on. Let's get you comfy and resting." Somewhere in a quiet corner so I can get a chance to think this through.

He follows me inside and forgets to take off his shoes. I poke him in the ribs—it's habit—and he glances down sheepishly. It seems like the old days. There're some things even amnesia can't take away.

He toes off his giant shoes and lines them up by the door.

"That better?" he teases.

Brushing my dark bangs from my eyes, I say, "I don't want nasty outside germs on my floor."

"Well, I don't want to have cold feet," he retorts.

"Your feet are always a million degrees." There's one particular hair that's stuck to my eyelashes. I can't find it. I blink rapidly.

Archie leans forward and gently pulls the hair away

from my eye. His calloused fingers brush against my eyebrow as he says, "It's a million degrees in this house."

You can say that again. "I get cold."

He turns around and heads into the living room, as though he didn't just set my heart racing. He stops abruptly, looking at the couch. I'm afraid he'll say something about it. Or maybe it will make him remember.

I turn to look in the entryway mirror and attempt to straighten my too-long bangs back into place.

Funny how it feels like I'm looking at a stranger in the mirror. Like I'm watching someone else in my own home. I still have the same long, dark-brown hair that's the exact shade of Archie's. My thick dark brows and eyelashes save me on the days I don't want to bother with makeup. My eyeliner is uneven, but I've resigned myself to never being a makeup aficionado. My white button earrings make me seem tanner than I really am.

"Wow!" Archie's exclamation pulls me away from my self-examination in the mirror.

I follow after with dragging steps.

"I could have sworn the couch was red."

I stare at the blue couch. I wanted to buy it, but he categorically refused. Said that he would not have a robin-egg-blue couch in his living room. We had fights about getting this couch. In fact, it was a star player in The Fight. When he left, I promptly went out and bought it.

"It looks nice!"

I wonder if I wrap my hands around his neck and squeeze, if it would make everything right in the world again. It might make *me* feel better—at least momentarily.

"Yeah, some things have changed."

The understatement of the year, I want to scream at him. I want to tell him that he hates this couch, that he left me and broke my heart. No, he didn't break my heart. He shattered it, then swept the pieces into a neat little pile and stomped on it.

I'm not sure I have any heart left. Maybe a little corner of it remained—the corner left to love my family. They'll always have a place. But maybe I love them with my being rather than my heart. That could be. Perhaps that is the difference between loves.

"Wow. Do you know how strange it is to..." Archie looks around the house, then finally sets Gatsby down.

I'll have a talk with that traitor later.

"It's so strange," he says. "I know I'm missing a big chunk of time, but it seems as though no time has passed. It scares me more that I might never remember those missing years."

My heart stutters at the thought. I assumed, at some point, his memories would return. *But what if they don't?*

"You still look sad. It's okay, Meyer," Archie says to me as he reaches out, latching my arm.

I freeze at his words. Sad that he doesn't remember? Sad at the possibility that he might never remember? Honestly, I don't know how I feel. I do know that I'm not ready for this physical closeness. I push out of his arms gently, careful of the stitches I know are close to his shoulder. It had been part of the discharge discussion.

I smile grimly, trying to figure out how to extricate my hand from his grasp without making it seem weird to him. "It makes me sad that you might miss those years."

He leans toward me and presses a kiss on my fore-head before I can get away. "Thanks, Meyer. I think I'll go shower and wash away the hospital grime."

I nod slowly, not bothering to mention the dried blood I see everywhere. "Okay. I'll get some dinner on."

He heads for the bathroom. And I'm glad I've been granted a reprieve—one that I am not going to waste. I pull out my phone and frantically text Bailey back again.

Me: Archie was the one flying that plane.

She might text back right away, or I might hear from her in three days. Bailey has young children, and I've come to learn that things get wild real fast when there are tiny humans running around. At one point, I walked into her house to find a child hanging from a doorjamb. He'd climbed up there himself while his mother had dared to go pee. I don't think she's made that mistake ever since.

I walk into the kitchen and open the freezer, looking for something to eat. When I'm by myself, I don't bother to cook. Why would I? Party of one, dismal eating and dining, please.

But Archie needs something healthy to help him heal. How much kale can you feed a person in a single meal? As if I have kale in my fridge. Please, I'm not a psychopath.

I'll make something with the frozen chicken breast, and I think I have a small bag of frozen green beans. It's not much, but it will have to do. Besides, he'll be gone soon, and I can go back to my comfortable non–guilt eating.

The green beans are defrosting on the counter. Bailey still hasn't texted back, and the chicken breast won't thaw in the microwave.

Willa's texted me twice more, and Gatsby sits on my feet, meowing repetitively. He's as bad as a dog when it comes to food. Anything that falls to the ground, he gobbles up like a starving tiger.

When Archie and I picked out Gatsby from the litter, he lured us in with his personable attitude and his zest for food. We thought it was cute that a kitten could eat so much. We were idiots. Gatsby ate more than Archie and I combined in his first year of life. As an adult, his voracious appetite eats away at my retirement fund because he consumes so much.

"Hey, honey." The voice startles me out of my memories of cat shopping with Archie.

I spin around to find Archie standing in my kitchen, wrapped in a peach-colored bathroom towel. I repainted the bathroom and picked out new linens a couple months ago. Now, I wish I'd gotten the extra-large towels because it barely reaches mid-thigh on Archie. Who knew kneecaps could be so scandalous? Especially considering I've seen all of him many, many times in the past.

"I can't find my shampoo in there. Do you mind if I use yours?" The front of his chest is damp, as though he stepped into the shower and then realized his shampoo was missing.

"Yes, I will grab you some more at the store. Go ahead and use mine," I manage to say.

His eyebrows shoot up. His hold on the towel relaxes, and it slips down a little. I choke.

"Wow, you must've been really worried that I was going to die if you're willing to let me use your shampoo."

I press my lips together in something that resembles a smile, and I hum my agreement.

Focus on the green beans, Meyer, not the naked man standing in front of you.

"If you can't find what you're looking for, go ahead and use what's there. It's not a big deal."

Somewhere in my head, a Morgan Freeman–style voice rings out, saying, *But it was a big deal.*

Or possibly a Clive Owen voice. Both are great options as a narrator.

Archie turns around and heads back to the shower. I watch as he walks away. His back muscles jump with each step. The tops of his hip bones are sticking out above the towel, and his bare feet slap loudly on the wood floor as he whistles a cheery tune.

I hope his memory comes back tonight. Possibly right now.

By the time I finish getting everything thawed and into a casserole dish, Archie walks out of the bathroom, rubbing the base of his neck as his eyes dart around the room. He's wearing that dang towel again, he probably smells like my shampoo, and he's looking at me like I am the stranger here.

"Where is all my stuff?"

"Huh?"

That dang doctor didn't have a suggestion for this.

There's no chapter in the *Heal Your Ex-Husband Manual* that covers this.

"Can you hold that thought for one minute?" I turn off the burner and move my cast-iron pan into the oven.

Then, I hurry outside, climb into my car, and shut and lock the doors. I pull out the little business card I stashed in the middle console and immediately punch in the number. I would hate making the phone call if it wasn't a pressing need.

"Hello? You've reached Dr. Sharpe."

"Hello, Dr. Sharpe. I am the ex-wife of your plane-crash patient."

I don't think I'll have to remind him of too many more details. We just left the hospital this morning, after all.

"Oh, hello, Mrs. Dunmore. What's up?"

Rather casual for an ER doctor, isn't he? And where does he come off calling me Mrs. Dunmore? Even if it is my name.

"You said that it would be best for him to recall everything himself."

There's a silence between us as he realizes that I need some type of confirmation for my nonquestion.

"That's correct. Usually, the less stress we add to a situation like this, the better."

"Then, we have a big problem. Because I'm about to add a lot of stress. He wants to know where all his stuff is, and I don't know how to explain it to him without telling him the truth."

"Could you be vague about it so that you don't plant any memories in his brain?"

"Plant memories?"

Hopefully, that isn't a thing. Archie might become convinced he's an adventurer. I can imagine him planting all sorts of his own outlandish memories.

"Yes. We want his memories to be completely his own. But if you were to tell him in general terms, he could understand the dynamic better. Perhaps you could tell him that you're not getting along well."

"Then, where would all of his stuff be? All I have is a few of his clothes he left behind in my guest closet."

"So, you kept those after the divorce?" His voice lilts with interest.

"I thought you were an ER doctor, not a psychoanalyst," I murmur.

He doesn't hear me over his thoughtful hum on the other end of the line. "You couldn't get his stuff back there by tomorrow?"

"No. It's a little difficult to do when he's from Arizona."

I don't mention that I still have things of his stashed in the garage. Old sketch pads. Pencils. Hiking boots. Maybe just a couple of things, really. Quite possibly multiple boxes. I'm sure it isn't strange that I'm hanging on to them. Not unhealthy at all.

There's an amused chuckle that is not very funny to me.

"It's up to you if you want to tell him the truth. I can't make that decision for you. I've given you my medical opinion, but sometimes, some things can't be helped, and permanent damage is collateral."

Permanent damage. Collateral. As though I want that on my conscience.

"Look, I've got to go, but feel free to call with any more questions," the doctor says.

"Thank you, Dr. Sharpe. And thank you for taking my call."

After the call ends, I set the phone on my leg. I stare through the windshield of my car toward the house. Archie is in the living room now, still wearing that towel. Hopefully, the neighbors can't see. Thank goodness all the lots in this neighborhood are at least an acre.

There's one more phone call I need to make. It's the solution to all my problems, and I should have made it earlier.

I pick up my phone again and dial the contact. Archie is picking up a picture frame off the mantel with one hand as he adjusts the towel with his other.

"Meyer?" the voice ends in a question. "Is that you, sweetie?"

"Hi, Holly. Yes, it's me."

A whoosh of a sigh blasts through the line. "How are you? I'm so glad you called. You've been on my mind so much. I wasn't sure if you wanted to hear from me or not. I didn't want you to think I'd abandoned you, but then I didn't want you to think I was pressuring you—"

"Holly!"

She stops.

"It's okay, really. I should have called you sooner than this. I was worried about the same thing."

My ex-mother-in-law is a unicorn in this world. There was no competition for her son's affection. She loved him and wanted him to have a wife who loved him, too. There was nothing petty about her relationship with me. Instead, it was a friendship I cherished.

But after Archie moved back to Arizona, I wasn't sure where that left me. So, I didn't call. And neither did she. I assumed she hated me.

But so far, she's holding the rage back—if it's there.

"I'm afraid we have a problem," I finally manage to say. "I'm sorry I can't talk long, but your son is standing in my living room, wearing my towel." *And nothing else.*

"I'm afraid I can't help you there, sweetie. There are some things a mother doesn't want to know about her children." Her loud laugh is grating on my ears.

"Holly, he was in an accident. His plane crashed here in Green Lake. I picked him up from the hospital because I'm still listed as his emergency contact."

"You're always so kind to people, even when it's difficult."

"He's been hurt, Holly!"

I wonder if her blasé attitude could rub off on me. It would mean less stress.

"Of course, sweetie. Is he okay?"

"A concussion, some stitches. A dislocated shoulder."

She clicks her tongue. "That's not too bad. He had worse accidents as a child."

"But wait, there's more." I pause as I prepare to explain things to her. Is there a way to soften the truth? Not exactly, so I blurt it out, "Retrograde amnesia. He doesn't remember the last two years. At all. He thinks we're still married."

"What?" The shock in her voice bleeds through, and I curse myself for delivering the news so callously.

This is a *mother*. She would be worried and confused as to what she could do to help. I need to tread lightly.

"He's fine. Besides a few bumps and bruises, he's fine. Perfectly fine." I really need to stop saying the word *fine*. No other word instills panic or overthinking quite as much as *fine*. "He had to have some stitches across a cut on his forehead and a small cut where a piece of glass got him on the shoulder. The doctor promised me they are all superficial wounds that will heal quickly. Even the stitches will dissolve on their own if he doesn't pull them."

I shift to get comfortable before I go on. "But I'm afraid to send him back home to Arizona by himself when I don't know the extent of what he remembers. I was hoping maybe you or one of the family could come pick him up and fly back with him." An image of him trying to remember where he lives at a layover does not make me want to send him home by himself. He could easily become a Tom Hanks remake of *The Terminal*.

"Oh my." She exhales loudly. "That's a lot to take in."

"Yes, I'm still processing as well."

She hums. "Let me talk with the family and see what we can get arranged."

"I can come pick you up from the airport tomorrow," I offer.

"Is there a rush? He's not being mean to you, is he? I've heard head injuries can change personality a lot."

"No! Of course not."

Archie is many things, but physical violence has never been in his repertoire.

"But he doesn't remember anything. He thinks we're still happily married."

"How sweet," Holly gushes. "Maybe this is a sign! This could be a chance to fix things!"

Did I say Holly was wonderful? I take it back. She's two buns short of a picnic.

"Holly, he left me. If I keep him here, that's pretty much the equivalent of kidnapping!"

"Did he scream and try to get away?"

This conversation is not going to happen.

"Holly, please come get your son."

She sighs heavily. "All right. I'm sorry. It just seems like fate has lent you a hand here. I have it on good authority that you haven't dated anyone since he left."

Mom. The dirty traitor.

She and Holly hit it off as friends at our wedding, the first time they'd ever met. They were the rowdiest guests at the wedding, having the time of their lives together. Of course they would keep in contact.

"What I have or have not done in the past year is irrelevant. Getting Archie home is the important thing."

"Of course. Poor thing. I'll text you as soon as I have a time!"

"Thank you, Holly." I'm relieved she's taking this seriously now. It's her son, for crying out loud.

I hang up the phone and pop open the car door with the alacrity of a condemned prisoner.

Through the living room window facing the driveway, Archie holds his hands in the air, as if asking, *What?*

I guess there's going to be no power nap today. Too bad. I could use it.

Walking inside slowly, I dread the conversation that I need to have. The question is if I want to risk damaging him further by telling the truth or telling some fibs to get him healing properly so that he can be on his way quicker.

I open the front door and step inside.

Archie turns to me and asks, "Why is the TV so small?"

"You decided you didn't like large screens."

There are some things I don't have to make up along the way. Some changes in this house actually were implemented by him.

He looks at me in shock with a dash of horror. The man was obsessed with watching soccer. (He'd never played, so I don't know where his obsession comes from.) But he likes to feel as though he's personally in the game with a huge TV. He can't grasp the fact that he's changed his mind on such a crucial thing.

"I know it's hard to believe, but you decided that you didn't like letting a screen run your life."

"But I'm going to need a magnifying glass to watch any movies on this thing."

I fight a grin, surprised at my slightly evil enjoyment of this. I could have a little bit too much fun with him not remembering certain things.

A different scenario floats across my mind of me doing exactly what the doctor recommended I don't do—implant certain memories in his mind. Tell him that, now, he's in the habit of cooking me a five-course dinner every night, that he visits Margaret every morning for coffee, that he loves going for a run every morning (Archie hates running).

I wonder if he would try to do those things in an effort to regain his memories...

My revenge fantasy will have to be just that—a fantasy. But I could always add to it in my mind, and there is potential in that. A therapeutic mental exercise.

I have a feeling the next day or two are going to be very long while I wait for his mother to come collect him.

It is the ultimate school drop-off moment. The hospital being the school, me being the after-school care, and his mother running late to come get him. Maybe I could charge an exorbitant late fee...

"Archie, why don't we sit down and talk a little bit?" My serious tone snaps him out of his mourning for his giant TV.

He nods and sits down on the robin-egg couch.

"Something has happened, hasn't it?" he finally says.

I should be worried that he'll figure it out, but I only feel relief. It would be nice to not have to hide anything. And while maybe it isn't best that he learns about our divorce this way, at least he put two and two together.

"What happened to my shampoo?"

"That's not important right now," I say. *Because if I tell you about the shampoo, you're going to realize everything is wrong.*

"What is it you want to tell me?" Before I can reply, his eyes widen more than I thought humanly possible. "We didn't have a baby, did we?" he practically yells.

I shake my head rapidly. Playing into that one would be too cruel. "No, no baby."

We'd had the kid conversation only twice in our marriage. We planned to revisit the conversation once we were both settled in our careers. We had two years of happy marriage, a year and a half of a slow slide into anger and disappointment, and now I was twenty-five and had already been divorced for a year. *'Young and in love'* is not the cure-all everyone says it is.

Archie's face relaxes. "I would hate to have missed that. A baby."

Maybe he wanted kids more than I'd realized. I can see his eyes darting around the room as though looking for answers. With no other recourse, I blurt it out, "We're fighting, Archie."

"I'm sorry. I know I'm getting loud, but I'm not trying to fight. I'm just trying to figure out what's going on," he explains as he spreads his legs and leans forward to rest his elbows on his knees. The towel gapes dangerously.

I drag my eyes back up to his face. "No, I mean, we're not doing well in our marriage."

Going with vague terms is going to be harder than I thought.

He taps his fists together as he processes this information. The towel shifts again, and I turn to stare at the tiny TV.

"What did we do?"

I shake my head for the millionth time today. "We don't need to focus on that right now. Now, you are the most important thing. Getting you healthy again. I wanted to explain why some things are...well, different right now."

A shadow crosses his face as he processes my words.

"We were so mad at each other that some of your things are in the guest room." I sink down onto the cream armchair.

"Wow," he whispers.

We sit in silence, and Gatsby jumps to the coffee table.

Finally, he speaks. "It's okay, Meyer. Whatever's wrong, whatever happened, we'll get through it. We always do."

If only he knew what I know.

"I need to go finish dinner. Why don't you try and take a nap? I'll wake you when it's ready."

"I don't need a nap. I'm not tired at all. Let me help you with dinner," he protests.

I stand up, and my ankle pops when I do so. "The doctor said you need rest. Please."

I'm not in the mood to argue with him, and I think he can see the exhaustion on my face.

"Fine. I'll lie down, but I probably won't be able to sleep."

He curls up on the couch, still wearing his towel. His petulant face almost makes me smile as I leave the room.

Chapter Four

Despite his protests that he didn't want to nap, Archie is out to the world on the robin-egg-blue couch right now—the one that looks just right in the living room.

Pulling the cast-iron dish out of the oven, I check the temperature. Chicken is a meat waiting to kill you if you don't cook it all the way. I stir the cooked chicken breast in the dish, then lower the temperature on the oven. A green-bean-and-chicken casserole is the only magic I can work up. I didn't plan on company.

I slice an onion to sauté on the stovetop.

At least Archie isn't picky. It's a redeeming quality of his. He's the better cook out of the two of us, but he never complained about the things I made. He'd lie and tell me it was the best meal he'd ever eaten, then promptly offer to cook the next meal.

As the onion sizzles, I peek at Archie to make sure he's still sleeping. He is.

I need to make a lifeline call. And then after that, I

will never speak on the phone again. My lifetime quota has been filled in one day.

I step into the laundry room and shut the door. Pulling out my phone, I call my sister, Bailey.

"Hello? Meyer? What's wrong? Are you okay?" she answers the phone with a frantic tone.

I don't call people—not if I can help it. She's right that something is wrong.

"Did you actually see the plane crash?" I ask.

"Yes." She pauses, and a small child yells in the background. "Have you talked to Margaret yet? I saw your text. You know who was flying."

"Yes," I whisper.

"Oh, good. I didn't want to be the one to tell you. I think he's fine, though, if you're worried about that."

"He's not fine." My voice cracks.

"Go play in the living room. I need to talk to Auntie Meyer right now."

I listen as she shoos the kids out of whatever room she's in.

Then, she zones in on me. "You know something. Tell me what happened."

Why do sisters have the ability to read minds? "He's in my house."

"He's what?" Her screech has me pulling the phone away from my ear.

"The hospital called me today. I didn't know about the plane crash, but they called me and told me my husband had been in an accident. I'm still his emergency contact, apparently."

"Why is he in your house? Is his neck broken?"

"No. His brain. Bailey, he has amnesia. He's forgotten the last two years. He thinks we're still married!"

Saying it out loud doesn't make it any less ridiculous in my mind.

"Stop laughing, Bailey."

She wheezes as she catches her breath.

"It's not funny!" I whisper-yell. I don't want to wake the subject of our conversation.

"What are you going to do?"

"I don't know! He thinks having sex will help him heal faster, Bailey!"

"Maybe it will..."

"Whose side are you on?" I ask.

She sobers quickly. "Yours, of course. It's strange, is all. You have to admit, only Archie would return to your life this way."

I walk to the back door and glance out the window to see Gatsby strolling around the base of my birdbath. An unsuspecting robin stands on the edge. If he's not careful, he'll end up a snack for a very fat cat.

"What did he say when you told him you were divorced?" Bailey asks. I can hear her coffeepot sputtering in the background.

"I...haven't told him."

There's silence on the other end, and I can hear her rooting through her extensive mug collection, looking for the largest one. Which reminds me...

"Are you hoping he won't remember?" she asks softly, pityingly.

"No!" I snap as I climb on top of my dryer to reach

the box on the top shelf. "No. The ER doctor thought he would heal faster if he was able to remember things on his own. He said big shocks weren't necessarily great for the healing process, which is why I called Holly, and she's going to come get him. I'm still trying to think up an excuse for why he should go stay with his family in Arizona. He doesn't remember leaving at all."

I climb down, careful not to drop the box.

"Poor guy," Bailey says sympathetically.

No matter how Archie hurt me in the past, I wouldn't have wished this on him. When his memories come back, I wonder if it'll jump him forward emotionally or if his feelings will still be stuck here, thinking we're happily married. Or if he would be confused and experience the emotional roller coaster of divorce a second time.

"Listen, I need you to talk to Margaret. He'll only be here for a day or two while we wait for Holly to catch a flight out here." I open the box and pull out his two favorite mugs, carrying them into the kitchen and giving them a quick rinse. I leave one in the dish rack and put the other one away in the cupboard.

"He's not five. Why not send him on the plane by himself?" Bailey asks. I can hear the clink of the coffeepot in the background as she pours her lifeblood into a mug.

"Because he's had a serious trauma. I'm scared to send him out into the world by himself. What if he forgot where he was going? It's still too soon to know exactly how this whole amnesia thing works. Archie gets lost on a regular day; sending him out into the world with retrograde amnesia could be detrimental."

I return to the laundry room and pull out his water bottle, stashing it in my messy cup cupboard.

"Good point. Well, what do you want me to tell Margaret?" Bailey asks.

"Ask her to be the head of the *Heal Archie Quickly* campaign. I need her to make sure no one mentions the *divorce* word and that they act like he didn't leave."

"What color would you like your carriage, Cinderella?" Her haughty tone would make me laugh on a regular day. Today is not a regular day.

"Please, Bailey. I just want to get him out of here as fast as possible with as little drama as I can. And I know you and Margaret can make sure everyone stays away." I open the small cupboard that acts as my pantry. I find the old coffee beans in the back and stick them next to the coffeepot. Year-old coffee beans? Does coffee get old? We're about to find out.

Archie hates canned coffee—which is what I drink. He would think it's strange if there were no coffee beans out on the counter for him.

"Ugh, fine. But you owe me."

"Thanks, sis. I've got to go check my casserole."

"Bibbidi-bobbidi-boo."

"You might need to cut back on the caffeine."

"Never," she growls before she hangs up.

Taking a deep breath, I step out of the laundry room and quietly make my way toward the living room again. He's still asleep.

Perfect. Extra time to make it seem like he still lives here.

"Thank you for dinner, Meyer. It was delicious."

The green-bean-and-chicken casserole was somewhere between burnt toast and the crispy fires of hell—the result of my conversation with Bailey and spending too long staring at my sleeping ex-husband in between laying things around the house that he'd left behind. I needed it to look lived in.

He mercifully put on a pair of sweats I'd found for him in the guest closet. Thank goodness. I don't know how much longer I could have looked at him in that bath towel.

It would have been pure torture to sit through dinner with him still wearing it.

Archie stands up and grabs his plate. He was always great at doing the dishes whenever I cooked.

"Go get in bed."

"Okay."

His quick agreement nearly makes me trip as I begin to clear the table.

"I can't believe I'm saying it, but I'm having a hard time keeping my eyes open, even after that nap." He stretches his neck to the side. "Do you think I have a lot of missed calls today? I can't believe I haven't checked my phone at all."

"Considering your mind is fighting to heal, you should probably just not worry about it. Anyone who needs you has my number, too," I reassure him, even though that's not quite true. "Besides it might not be a good idea to look at your phone yet. It might shock something in your mind."

"It makes my head spin, thinking of trying to explain this to people. As long as there's nothing pressing, I think I'll avoid my phone until everything makes sense again." He presses the heel of his hand to his forehead. "It won't stop spinning."

"It's your brain telling you that it needs sleep and time to heal," I remind him as I pick up the casserole dish. I might need a jackhammer to chisel out the leftover chicken breast.

I'm grateful I didn't have to fight him over the phone. What if he saw that we haven't called or texted each other at all in the last year? That would have been a little awkward to try and explain away.

"I'm trying so hard to remember, but it's like this dark hole. Leave the dishes. I'll do them in the morning." He stands up and heads to the bathroom.

I freeze as I realize he's still stuck in the moment of two years ago. Back when he wasn't too busy to do the dishes. What if the memories never come back? I'm hopeful he'll be healed and on his way in the morning... but that's not a guaranteed thing.

"Where's my toothbrush?" he calls from the hallway.

"I cleaned the bathroom this morning!" Truth. I did clean the bathroom this morning, but that fact has nothing to do with him not being able to find his toothbrush right now. "Check in the drawer! I have extra toothbrushes there."

He disappears into the bathroom, and I sprint through the house at a dead run. I was limited with how many of his things I could set out while he was sleeping. Our house is small, and you can see most of the rooms from the living room. He could have woken up to find me carrying things back and forth. I fling open the door to the garage and frantically grab a box off the shelf. I carry it to my room and rip it open.

I pull out his old razor and a coat.

I run and hang up the coat by the front door and stick the razor by the laundry room sink. With only one bathroom in the house, it was common for him to shave in the laundry room with the big sink and mirror hanging there.

With a quick peek down the hall to make sure he's still in the bathroom, I run back to the box and pull out his old sketch pads and pencils.

I sprinkle them in strategic locations around the living room and kitchen. Placing drawing pencils in the junk drawer, I lay the erasers on top.

Running back to the box, I pull out a couple baseball caps and a pair of old running shoes and shove them in my closet. Unfortunately, I never had the guts to throw out the clothes he left behind in my dresser. The four drawers are still completely full of his things.

I pull out his hiking boots and stick them on the boot rack by the front door and hope that he isn't observant enough to realize that the boots weren't there when he first walked in.

Just as I finish shoving the box under my bed, I hear the bathroom door slam open. It does that periodically. I should get it fixed. I plant my hand against the bed and start to stand up when my eyes catch on my bare left hand. My ring.

Frantically reaching into my nightstand, I pull out my wedding and engagement rings and shove them on. It's a tight fit. The fact that I've slept with them right next to my bed probably does not speak well of how I'm handling the divorce.

I hurry out to the living room and watch as a very sleepy Archie walks out of the bathroom and stumbles toward my bedroom.

No way. That is not going to happen.

I was willing to do a lot of things to not rock the boat. Not shake the cradle. Whatever that saying is.

But let him sleep in my bed? No. I can't pretend that much. I run after him just as he crosses the threshold and pulls his shirt over his head.

He's reaching for the drawstring tie on his sweats as I skid into the room. I've been running for the last five minutes, and I'm winded. Cardio is not my thing.

My shaky hands automatically latch onto his. "Whoa there, cowboy. You're a little quick on the draw there."

He looks at me with mild amusement. "I thought you said that wouldn't be good for my head..."

"I'm not—I'm—" I yank my hand away, realizing I was touching him.

"I think I'll be fine," he says with a slow grin.

I jump back a few feet, and the backs of my legs bump against the bed. *Not the bed.* I scurry around the far edge and point to the door as I sputter, "You're sleeping in the guest room."

The look of surprise on his face could be from the news I delivered or from the fact that I snapped it out like a command. I am not a snapper by nature—or by any other force, for that matter. It takes my ex-husband trying to sleep naked in my bed to panic me into yelling.

"I think it would be better all-around if you slept in the guest room. I don't want you to be jostled," I suggest in a milder tone.

He saunters slowly around the edge of the bed toward me, the room growing smaller by the second. I now know what a sardine feels like.

"Won't you be worried about me not waking up if I sleep in the other room?"

I swallow the lump in my throat and stare at anything but his naked chest. "It's just that you haven't been—well, you haven't been—" His hand is reaching for me, and I belt out, "The fight!"

His teasing look fades away. "Oh, right. I'm sorry, Meyer. I really wish I could remember what we were fighting about so I could fix it."

I smile faintly at that. "Thank you. It's best this way. Until you're healed."

And out of my life.

Why did that thought leave me feeling empty?

He nods slowly and shuffles out of the room, looking like I just kicked him. I have the sudden urge to invite him to sleep in my bed, but I know he'll thank me for this later—when he remembers everything.

Chapter Five

I wake the next morning to the smell of breakfast. A home-cooked breakfast. I haven't smelled that in over a year. It immediately takes me back in time, and I'd rather not unpack the warm feeling in my chest at the moment.

The strong aroma of coffee wafts through the air. Gatsby is sitting on the end of my bed. There is an indent on the pillow next to me. The bed is rumpled. And I usually sleep in the same position all night.

Surely, he didn't sneak into bed last night? I thought I'd made it clear that we had been fighting. I shudder to think what else might've happened in the middle of the night.

I prepare to climb out of bed—because I have to prep my mind for the cold floor. I don't like sleeping in socks. But I also don't like to step out onto a cold floor.

One of these days, I will have to make the adult decision to buy a pair of slippers. It feels like one of those over-the-hill crossings. But I have to admit, I'm at the point in my life where I prefer comfort over style.

Ugly-ass slippers coming right up. But before I throw back the covers, the bedroom door opens, and in strolls Archie. He's not wearing a shirt.

His body temperature usually runs a little warmer than the average. I used to appreciate this about him, but now it seems like a glaring flaw designed to distract me.

The stitches high on his shoulder look less inflamed this morning.

He has a plate of breakfast in his hands. I sink my bottom teeth into my top lip. Seeing him walk into our bedroom as though nothing were amiss, I want to leap on him and drag him back to bed with me. I also want to kick him in the ass. I'm not sure which out of the two I prefer. But most likely, neither of those options.

Instead, I say, "What's that you have there?"

He smiles and extends the plate to me. "I woke up early this morning and made breakfast."

He sets the plate on my lap, then backs up a step, smiling at me. He's giving me space, and it's rather sweet. There's an omelet on the plate, and it smells divine. Gatsby agrees, of course, and prowls up the bed.

"Oh no, you don't," I tell the cat. "I am not sharing a bite of this with you."

I immediately cut into the omelet, taking a huge bite. "Hot, hot, hot."

Archie grimaces. "I'm sorry. I should've warned you."

"This is divine." I close my eyes and enjoy the taste now that my mouth isn't on fire.

"I'm glad you like it," his voice rumbles.

Something scratchy touches my wrist. My eyes fly

open, and I scowl at Gatsby, his guilty cat tongue reaching out to lick me once more.

"Don't you do it. This won't get me to share with you." My words don't jive with my hands as I break off a very small corner of the omelet and give him a nibble. "Now, that's it. You've had a taste, and you can go catch a mouse or something since you're so determined to be an outdoor cat."

Gatsby ignores me and starts kneading my leg with his claws.

I eat half the omelet, then turn to Archie, who's leaning against the doorframe. "Are we going to talk about the fact that you slept in my bed last night? Or should I say, that you snuck into my bed last night?"

He grins and rocks back on his heels, shoving his hands into his sweatpants pockets. His ab muscles harden as he engages them. There's a beginning of a bruise across his lower abdomen, and I wonder if it's from the seatbelt.

"Nope," he replies cheerily.

I shake my head, not ready to ruin this delicious breakfast. It's been a while. A lot of times, I don't even think about breakfast—not for breakfast time, anyway.

I love having an omelet for dinner. I'm a firm believer in BFD—breakfast for dinner—at any opportunity. But Archie loves a good breakfast for *breakfast*. Absolutely horrifying, if you ask me, which is why I'm shocked that he was able to find enough ingredients to make an omelet.

"I'll go grab your coffee," Archie says.

"I think I'm supposed to be serving you food," I reply around a very large mouthful of omelet, remembering the stale coffee beans.

He shrugs the shoulder without the stitches. "You know I like doing it."

I fight the urge to turn that into a dirty joke, because I think he'd be more than willing. He taps his hand against the doorframe and walks out of the room, leaving the bedroom door wide open. I can see him walk into the kitchen and open the cupboard, not finding the mugs because I moved them three months ago. But he doesn't ask me where. He searches the cabinets until he finds them, pours me a cup of black coffee, and shuffles back into the room.

I watch him walk, realizing that he's favoring one of his legs. Any accident that could rob a man of his memories had to be enough to severely bruise and batter the rest of him—and probably not just surface bruises.

I jump out of bed and hurry toward him. I take the coffee mug out of his hands and then point to the couch. "Sit down."

His eyebrow shoots up at that. I don't boss people around. Not usually. Gatsby is the only object of my dictator-role tendencies, and even that gives me very little results.

But for some reason, knowing that Archie needs someone to take care of him makes it easier for me to tell him what to do. "You need to go sit down right now. I saw you limping across the room."

I put a hand on my hip and take a sip of the hot black coffee. I panic-swallow the steaming liquid. I am going to have a fuzzy tongue tomorrow—I'm sure of it. Two times, I've underestimated the temperature of something I put in my mouth. At least I won't be able to taste the old coffee.

Archie leans toward me and smirks. "I think I like this bossy mouth on you."

"Then, you're going to like me a whole lot more because, obviously, someone needs to tell you what to do to heal your body."

He runs a hand through his hair, sending it shooting in all different directions. The sides are short, and the top is a little longer. It's not his usual haircut. But it still looks amazing on him.

"Now," I snap at him and try my best to fold my arms across my chest while holding the mug.

His grin threatens to split his face as he turns and walks into the living room, sitting down in the center of the couch.

"Happy now?" he asks, stretching his arms along the back of the couch and manspreading.

"Yes. As long as you promise not to leave that spot. And not to sneak into my bed again."

He has the decency to look guilty. "I was serious when I said I want to fix whatever it is between us. I know I need to remember things on my own, but it doesn't mean we have to freeze in time. Life is still moving forward even if my mind isn't. And to you, what-ever we argued about must've been a big deal. And I want to fix it for you."

I walk to the TV and grab the remotes off the shelf, tossing them onto the couch next to him, resisting the urge to reach out and touch him. "The best way to fix us is to fix you."

Such a loaded statement. One that I mean very much in a literal sense.

I head to the kitchen and grab a second mug—his mug I frantically stashed in the cupboard last night. I fill it almost halfway with milk—the way he likes it.

I walk back into the living room and hand it to Archie.

"Thank you. I love milk." His eyes are sparkling.

I glance into the mug.

"Crap." I grab the mug out of his hands and march back into the kitchen. I forgot to add the coffee.

His laugh follows me, not that it's hard in this house.

"What time is it?" he calls.

I glance at the clock. "Seven-thirty," I call back as I set the coffeepot back into place.

"I'd better call into work, then, shouldn't I?"

My brain runs through an invisible calendar in my mind. He would've been working at the finance firm.

"You don't work there anymore."

"Good for me!" He slaps a hand on his knee as I walk back to him with a cup of coffee.

"I have to go get ready for work."

"You're still working at the real estate office, right?"

The rational part of my brain knows Archie is trying to organize the information. But the irrational part—which I'm beginning to think has overtaken my entire mind—is screaming that he thinks my worth is tied up in that job. Because that was a big part of our separation—the careers that took so much of our time.

"I'm actually working from home now. But I have a meeting with someone first."

He looks skeptical. But he doesn't say anything. Just sips his coffee. "You run a realtor business from home?"

"No...I've turned M's Buttons into a full-time gig," I reply quietly.

His eyes widen, but he doesn't frown. Even if he did remember everything, he wouldn't have known about this. I quit the realty office after the divorce. M's Buttons became my full-time job a month after he left.

My Grandma had been an earring fiend when she was alive. Big earrings, every. Single. Day. It was something I had loved as a child. She was someone I aspire to be as an adult. One of her signature pair of earrings was a big pair of button earrings—a pair that she gave to me when she caught me admiring them. I figured, why not make more of those for myself? And so I'd made my own collection of various colors.

In making earrings for myself, I learned that I enjoyed the crafting stage. Next, I discovered that other people enjoyed the unique take on post earrings and wanted a pair for themselves.

Eventually I took the leap to open an online shop. It did better than I expected.

What had started as a hobby inspired by my grandma had quickly become something I wanted to spend every spare minute on.

When I first went full time with M's Buttons, it was a scary month of relying on my meager savings, but I was glad for the business to pour my time and energy into. I didn't want time to think about my divorce. Not to mention, I was burnt out by my real estate job when I made the switch. M's Buttons had soothed my soul.

"What should I do while you work?" Archie asks, surprising me by not pursuing the subject of my career change.

"Read a book."

"Meh, I don't know where my reading glasses are."

I know exactly where they are. In his apartment in Arizona. But I am sure I saw an extra pair floating around here. I'll have to go on a discreet search. "Binge-watch TV."

He glances back at the small TV. "I'll still need my reading glasses. Maybe a telescope."

I glare at him, stomp forward, grab a high-backed dining room chair, and carry it back to the living room. I plop it down directly in front of the TV. "Knock yourself out. I'll be back in an hour. You are to be resting. *Resting*, you hear me?"

He crosses his heart and nods solemnly. "R and R only."

"Oh, and you should probably call your mom. I talked with her yesterday. I think she'd like to know that you're okay."

"Do you know where my phone is?"

I point to the plastic bag sitting by the front door. The hospital staff bagged up all personal effects that had been on his person when he arrived. "I left a charger in the kitchen."

"Thanks, Meyer. I'll call mom then turn it off again."

I let out a relieved sigh, then turn around and hurry to the bedroom.

After getting ready in record time, which involved combing my bangs in a similar direction and putting my earrings on, I hurry out of the house.

Closing the front door reduces my heart rate immediately. Hopefully, by the time I return this afternoon, his memory will be back, and everything will be fine. He'll probably be gone by the time my meeting finishes. With that hope in mind, I drive to The Egg Crack, a breakfast bistro. I planned on eating brunch with my PR manager, but I'm full after that delicious omelet Archie made. I guess I'll have to make do with a breakfast espresso.

"You made it."

Willa acts like I'm late. I glance at my watch—I am. She looks delightfully put together. She doesn't fight a losing battle with bangs. Instead, it's a smooth low bun that looks classy. How does she manage it?

"What do you want for breakfast? I already ordered. I hope that's okay. I was starving, and I thought it would take you a while to get here."

I'm not that late, but I don't say anything. Willa can sometimes be slightly feral when hungry, so it's best to not get between her and food. A waiter comes over to our table, and I ask for a shot of espresso.

Then, I turn to Willa, and she sets her laptop on the table, flipping it open. She dumps a few packets of sugar into her coffee mug.

"I emailed you the ads report. I also updated our newsletter schedule. If you could give me some personal tidbits, I'd like to push a piece into some magazines. It would be really good exposure for you."

The waiter comes back with my espresso. He also sets a little cup of cream next to my steaming cup.

"Thank you."

Willa taps away on the laptop, and then she rests her elbows on the table, folding her hands together.

She has a big grin on her face. *Always scary.*

"I have big news. Huge news." She throws her hands in the air.

I forgot about her text yesterday. In the midst of the chaos, I didn't think much about what her big news could mean.

"Well, I hope it's good news." I pour a little dash of cream into the espresso, not wanting it to be watered down too much.

"I approached Blanchett about acquiring your brand. They're writing up an offer right now."

I set the creamer down with a clink. Blanchett. Blanchett is a direct competitor of Nordstrom.

"What do you mean, acquire my brand?"

"I mean, they would sell your earrings. The demand could push you into heavier production."

"Oh, wow, Willa. I'm impressed that you got through to them." I don't know what else to say. I didn't ask her to do this. It seems to be the next logical step for growing a business, but it has literally never crossed my mind.

"I know, right? This is incredible. You know that saying, *It's not what you know; it's who you know?* Well, it's right. My uncle manages the Oregon branches and was able to extend the offer. But don't think he's doing it as a favor. He's a strict businessman. If it won't profit him, he won't do it. I've had my phone on the loudest possible volume all week, waiting for the call."

"You knew about this for a week, and you didn't tell me?"

She waves her hand through the air. "I didn't want you to be disappointed if it didn't go through. Like I said, my uncle isn't a pushover."

For some reason, I feel like I'm at my first piano recital all over again—sweaty, slippery fingers and the back of my dress caught in my tights. A trauma my five-year-old mind never lets me forget. Taking a deep breath, I remind myself there is no stage and only one audience member.

I know Willa worked hard on this. That is one thing you can always count on her for. She goes the extra mile. She's been a huge asset to my business.

"There's so much to think about."

"I know. You're probably in shock. But I have lots of other things to discuss with you while you sip your espresso. Don't let your mind jump too far forward on the Blanchett deal because I don't have a definite answer yet."

I spend the next hour chatting with Willa about the actual business side of my business. She's very good at that part.

My sister, Bailey, convinced me to hire someone who enjoyed the business, marketing, admin side of my earring business. I shuddered, thinking about those things, and I knew if I wanted to make a living selling my earrings that I would need her help. Willa has quickly increased my profit, and I get to keep creating.

As I leave the bistro, I realize I don't feel refreshed. The Blanchett deal makes my arms tingle. Is it a good thing? Interest from a company that huge is a compliment in itself. But am I ready to let M's Buttons go commercial?

I stuff my frantic questions into a special lockbox I've labeled *Pull Out When in Need of Anxiety*.

Instead, I focus on getting home and getting to work on doing what I love—creating.

Chapter Six

Archie is busy napping when I get home from The Egg Crack, so I check his pulse, make sure he is actually sleeping, then disappear into my office for a few hours. When I emerge, Archie is sitting on the couch that has mysteriously been moved closer to the TV and is watching a documentary on ocean life.

The front door swings open.

No knock, no warning, but the wave of noise that blasts me leaves no doubt about who it is.

Several small blurs run inside the house.

One of them yells, "Uncle Archie!"

Archie mutes the TV and immediately stands up. He takes a step forward and drops to his knees, holding his arms out. My nephew fist bumps him before racing to the basket of toys I keep under the coffee table.

My niece jumps into his arms and places a smacking kiss on his cheek. I hold my breath as I wait to hear what she says. She's young enough that she might not have paid attention to the time that he's been gone. She's also young enough to blurt out things like the truth.

"I missed you, Uncle Archie."

"I missed you, too, pumpkin."

I try not to let any emotion sweep through me at the choked-up sound in his voice. Two years are missing in his mind, so the three-year-old is now five. Elijah, only eleven months younger, probably does not remember him as clearly, which is why toys take precedence.

"That's why I hurried back to you on my plane. I probably crashed because I was trying to land in your backyard."

She laughs and wiggles out of his arms. "Uncle Archie, my yard isn't big enough for a plane." She leans a little closer and tries to whisper, "But it is big enough for a pony."

Bailey rolls her eyes at Lily's obvious ploy. She greets me with a hug, and I don't know if I want to hug her back or strangle her. I've spent a few hours hiding in my office, working, while Archie napped and attempted to watch TV quietly because he didn't want to disturb my creative process.

Archie stands up and looks at Leo, the baby. "Who is this?"

"Silly Archie." Lily laughs.

Bailey smiles softly at him. She's always gotten along really well with Archie—something I was grateful for. Archie has always endeared himself to my family. And I think, sometimes, they might blame me more for our separation. Some of them operate under the correct assumption that I was the one who drove him away, though they've never said it to my face.

"This is Leo Archie Potter."

Archie's eyes widen at that. "Just Archie?"

Bailey grins. "Just Archie."

Archie smiles softly at Leo and extends his hand toward him. Leo promptly grabs a large finger and pulls it toward his mouth.

Archie always talked about why someone should name their kid Archie, but never ever Archibald. He is not a fan of the name he was saddled with, and Archie is a byproduct of that.

Archie retrieves his finger from Leo, who grins at him. "I didn't even know."

"It's okay," Bailey said. "You'll remember."

"Anyone want a popsicle?" I ask to break the tension.

Everyone ignores me, even the kids.

"It's good to see you," Bailey starts to say, but I kick her in the shin with the back of my heel. "Alive," she adds with a glare in my direction. "It looked like it was a bad wreck." Bailey said.

Archie nods. "Thank you, Bailey. Hopefully, I don't do that again, whatever it was I did. Did Meyer tell you about—" He gestures awkwardly toward his head. "I'm assuming she did."

"Yes, she told me. Dan wanted to come say hi right away, but he had to work today."

"That was nice of him," Archie said.

Dan and Archie always got along, and we regularly did things with them as couples. Less frequently after they had four hundred kids, but it was still a fun time whenever we could.

I haven't done much with friends since Archie left. It feels too strange to go be the single one, especially in a group of friends who were friends with my ex-husband as well. I'm not completely sure that I wouldn't receive some type of condemnation from them. And I am not in a good enough space to handle that kind of conversation.

"I spoke with Margaret before I came over here." Bailey looks at me pointedly.

I give a single nod.

Bailey continues, "I barely convinced her to stay home with her casserole dish."

Archie chuckles at that.

"She wanted to feed you so badly," Bailey said.

"She's a good one," Archie says.

Meanwhile, I take a deep breath as I realize I've barely avoided a disaster. Margaret in my house with Archie? That could end so badly. If you want to talk about a ticking time bomb, that woman is it. She knows everyone's secrets, and she isn't like a bank vault that keeps everything locked up tight. She's more like a misfiring sprinkler, scattering information who knows where.

Small hands tuck into mine, and I'm led into the kitchen by two voraciously hungry children who seem to have finally recognized the word *popsicle*.

Nothing will stave off their hunger, except for a popsicle. Popsicles I keep specifically for my niece and nephew—soon-to-be nephews, as baby Leo is beginning to realize he is missing out on something yummy in the kitchen. He knows, whatever it is, it puts a big grin on his siblings' faces, and it won't be long before he toddles in and demands one of his own.

It makes me nervous to think about leaving Bailey in the living room with Archie. Them being together doesn't make me nervous, but rather what she might say, or what he might ask her to reveal.

I know he's trying to understand what is going on. There's so much that has changed in two years, and he's trying to connect the dots.

I check my phone to see if Holly has called me back. I tried calling on my way home from my meeting with Willa, but I still haven't heard back from her. I wonder if Archie got through to her. I forgot to ask.

Hopefully, this means she's in the air right now and about to get here. That would be a relief. I shoot off a quick text to her.

Me: Are you almost here?

Then, I focus on getting popsicles out of the freezer for two kids who are waiting patiently.

"What color do you want?" I ask.

We have an in-depth discussion on the merits of a red versus purple popsicle, and it's about to turn into an argument when I intervene.

"It's okay because red and purple are the best flavors of popsicles."

"Mom likes the yellow ones," Lily pipes up as she licks the red popsicle.

"Dad says they give him heart freeze," Elijah adds.

"Do you mean brain freeze?" I ask him.

He hums in agreement.

"Yeah, that's what I said." Elijah looks at me as though I misplaced my understanding of the English language.

Bailey steps into the kitchen and points at the kids. "Aren't you supposed to be sitting at the table while you eat those?"

The mom look has them scurrying to my kitchen table. I have to fight a laugh.

Bailey stops next to me and asks in a whisper, "When does Holly get here?"

"She hasn't called me back yet. So, I'm hoping that means she's nearly here." I glance at the clock on the oven. It's been eighteen hours since I spoke with her.

"Can you get flights that fast?"

Considering the fact that I spent many hours staring at flight plans from Oregon to Arizona, I know that same-day flights are one hundred percent possible. Did I try to book one of those same-day flights to chase after my ex-husband? No. No, I didn't. That would have been pathetic—and exactly something I debated about doing.

"After you finish those popsicles, we need to go, kids."

"Oh, do we have to?" Lily whines.

"Yes," she says firmly. "We still need to go to the grocery store."

"Can I be the one to put things in the cart?" Elijah asks with a dangerous glint in his eye.

"Sure thing, honey."

I shake my head, recalling the one time I made the mistake of taking my nephews and niece grocery shopping with me. "You're a brave woman."

Bailey cackles. "No, I'm a tired one. Or some things

aren't worth the fight. And if they want to help me, I don't want to stop them."

Archie makes his way into the kitchen, still limping slightly. He really should be in bed, resting. He's ignoring sound advice from the doctor and me.

It feels like I'm trying to housebreak a cat—except worse. Gatsby didn't take much time at all. But Archie seems to refuse to listen to instruction. Whether it's mine or the doctor's. Maybe I *should* send him on a plane back home by himself and say to hell with it. But I know I can't do that.

"Did I hear someone is going to the grocery store without me?" he asks in the big, angry voice, making the kids laugh.

"I'm going to help put things in the cart!" Elijah declares, as though he's making sure no one's trying to take that privilege from him.

"And I'm going to drive the cart," Lily pipes up.

Leo is sitting on Archie's hip, looking happy as a clam, patting his shoulder repeatedly. Archie makes it look so natural.

"Isn't he just the cutest thing?" Archie asks me as he comes to stand next to me. His elbow brushes against my arm as the baby grins up at Archie and pats his cheek.

I find myself smiling at him genuinely. Because he's right. Leo is the cutest thing ever. The most kissable cheeks. The happiest little grin. The way he seems to have taken to Archie right away. It makes me realize Archie deserves a chance at his own happiness, too.

It's not fair of me to keep him trapped in the in-between, no matter how much I am tempted. I will do whatever it takes to help him remember.

After a sloppy popsicle-eating frenzy, Bailey herds the brood out the door.

The house seems oddly still and quiet with them gone. I switch the laundry, then walk into the living room to find Archie standing there, holding Gatsby.

"Do you think we could go look at the wreckage? I'm a little sad that I don't remember what happened. And they told me that it's my plane out there. Not one I chartered."

"We already did look at it."

Staring at wreckage that almost killed Archie isn't my idea of a good time. When I heard that Archie had bought a plane six months ago—thank you, social media— I actually cried. I knew something like this would happen.

"Just a drive-by. I'd like to go see what I had with me in the plane, then see what was wrong with the plane possibly."

"But—" I stop when I see the forlorn look on his face.

"Please. There are so many gaps. I just want everything to come back. Even if it's as simple as remembering that I bought a plane."

And maybe a visit there would make everything come back.

I wonder what he'll do when he does remember— probably run out of here, screaming and accusing me of being a kidnapper, holding him hostage in this house.

That's what I would do, anyway.

I top off Gatsby's food in the laundry room, as if he's

actually starving. And then I grab a sweatshirt off the hook.

Number one rule of Oregon life: never leave home without a coat of some kind.

"Leo Archie?" Archie asks as he follows me outside, carrying one of his old sweatshirts he left at the house. "I have a baby named after me?"

We climb into the car and shut our doors at the same time.

I smirk as I recall what got him that baby named after him. Hopefully, this is a safe memory to share with him. "You drove Bailey to the hospital when she was in labor. Dan was at work, and I was in Portland. She said you were traumatized from her yelling at you in the car."

The horrified look on his face is pure gold. "I wasn't in there, right?"

I shake my head. "Dan met you guys at the hospital, but I think the drive was enough to scar you for life."

Archie sits quietly as I turn into Margaret and Bailey's neighborhood. "Is it bad I hope I never recover that memory?"

I can't stop the giggle that sneaks out as we pull up in front of Margaret's house.

My laugh dies when I spot the top of the plane in the backyard. I know Margaret is home because her car is in the drive, meaning I'll probably have to go talk with her first and make sure that Bailey has explained everything to her. I can't be too safe with this. Holly has got to be here soon. Her text said that she'd be here soon. I wish she had bothered to give me a specific time.

I shut off the car and follow Archie to the house.

He knocks on the door with the assurance of a man who doesn't remember anything. Archie doesn't remember that Margaret is still upset that she played the piano at our wedding that didn't last. Yet another reason I'm hoping that Bailey explained the situation completely to her.

I can't afford any slips.

The door opens, and Margaret is standing there with a screwdriver in her hand. She looks directly at Archie. "Hello, you poor dear. Why don't you come in?"

"I hear I owe you some serious landscaping," Archie says as we walk inside the house.

The warm smell of cinnamon floats through the air. A candle is burning on the center of a tablecloth-covered oak table. The floral curtains have hung in this house so long that they've been in style multiple times.

An old, upright piano, which has absorbed the tears of hundreds of children, sits along the living room wall, with a rickety wood bench that I know creaks every time you lean too far forward.

"I was wondering if we could head into the backyard and take a look at the wreck."

Margaret's eyebrows shoot up at that. "You're asking my permission? I wish you had thought to ask before you parked your plane on top of my rhododendron bush."

I bite my lip to keep from smiling at the scolding she's giving Archie.

Margaret sets down the screwdriver next to a robot vacuum on the table. That doesn't look like it will end well, but I don't plan on interfering.

"Didn't Meyer tell you? I can't remember anything. Maybe I did ask your permission," he teases.

Margaret's the one fighting a smile now. "Cheeky boy. Do you know that you're the second person I've met who's had amnesia?"

"Are you sure I'm not the third? Because you didn't just meet me. You've known me for years."

Margaret's eyes narrow, and I cough discreetly.

"My great uncle fell off a windmill and completely forgot that he was married and had ten kids. They found him at the beach."

"Are we sure he had amnesia?" Archie asks dryly. "Maybe he just needed a vacation."

Margaret smacks the back of my hand when I have the audacity to laugh at his joke. I thought I was out of striking distance.

"Do you know what cured him of the amnesia?"

We both dutifully shake our heads.

"A knock on the head. I think the same could work for you, too." She stares at the top of Archie's head, as though contemplating the best spot for a hit.

Archie takes a sliding step backward. "As thrilling as that sounds, I think I'm going to have to pass on the cure."

"Oh, I don't know. If it works, then..." I throw out, and I catch the gleam in Margaret's eyes.

Archie reaches over and rests a hand on my lower back and says dryly, "You're hilarious, Meyer. Let's go look at the plane."

He carefully keeps me between him and Margaret as he guides us through the house toward the back door. Margaret follows behind.

Out of the corner of my eye, I spot Margaret picking up a large vase from her kitchen counter.

"Are you coming out to pick flowers?" I ask, halting any harebrained idea she might have.

"No, just rearranging my collection." She slides three jars back and forth in a mimicking of the shell game.

We continue past the hutch displaying her collectible dishes. Archie's hand burns an imprint on my back. I'll have a permanent tattoo of his palm.

I hurry forward, opening the door and stepping into the backyard.

The rose bed is still perfectly mulched, every bush trimmed into as uniform of a shape a rose bush could get.

The yard is mowed to a reasonable height, still long enough to be soft if you were to lie on it, not long enough to lose a bocce ball—if Margaret were the bocce-playing type. And she is. An absolute menace during a bocce game. Her yard-game nights are legendary, and most people would do almost anything for an invitation.

The serenity of the perfectly manicured yard is ruined by the back fence, shattered and splintered; the deep ruts streaking through the grass; and the airplane, bent around the downed tree—the tree that was standing before it met its fate with a steel death trap. This is why people were meant to be on the ground on their own two feet.

Staring at the plane, I relive every argument we ever had over him flying a little plane everywhere. Flight school had been an anxious time in my life. He knew that I would never ever set foot in one of those things.

I've flown commercially. Once. I rented a car and drove it back rather than getting on the return flight.

"No wonder I hurt." Archie rubs a hand up and down his shoulder and stares at the wreckage, a glazed look in his eye as he slowly limps forward.

"What are you doing?" I ask as I trail after him.

"I want to look inside and see if I can figure out what went wrong or if there's something that will help me remember." The determination in his eyes is a little frightening.

"You're not climbing up there when you're still hurt."

He waves a hand through the air. "It will be fine."

Five minutes later, and it is declared that he is not fine. He tore his stitches close to his collarbone, trying to climb into the plane, his leg is still too injured to bear his full weight, and the world is spinning around him.

"I'll be right back," I tell him after I guide him to the bench next to the rose bushes.

I march back to the plane and study it. It's crumpled and never going to fly again. That's the only reason I would even consider climbing inside.

Grateful for the barre workouts, I plant my hands on either side of the door, and with a jump, I pull myself into the plane.

My heart beats off rhythm for a few seconds, but I remind myself this airplane will not be soaring through the air ever again. *Nothing to fear.*

I survey the damage. I can't tell him what I'm looking at because all I see are a bunch of broken glass pieces and speedometers. I'm pretty sure all the gauges are there to tell you how fast the plane is going.

There's a duffel bag and a satchel on the ground. The duffel bag is zipped tightly, but the satchel is open, its contents spilled out. I squat down, careful not to cut myself as I stand the bag up.

"Are you okay in there?" Archie calls.

A tablet is facedown along with a sketch pad and a pack of what I know are his pencils. A water bottle, three granola bars, and a pack of gum are attempting to sneak out of the satchel as well.

I tuck them carefully back in, and my fingers brush against something that's rubber.

I know that texture. I pull out a small rubber avocado with a smiley face on it.

I stare at it for a full second before I drop it back in the bag like it's hot.

"I'm coming!" I croak out when I hear Archie call out to me again.

I carefully lift the satchel out of the broken glass. I toss the duffel bag out the open door, then loop the satchel over my shoulder as I hop down to the grass and mud below. Margaret will probably send Archie a yard maintenance bill later when the plane gets removed. Or even worse, she'll probably send me the bill.

"Maybe there's something here that will help you," I suggest breathlessly.

Archie is standing there, a trickle of blood trailing down his arm from under his shirtsleeve.

"I was worried you'd get cut in there. I didn't want you going in there and getting hurt." He's glancing over me as he checks for injuries. "Everything okay?"

"Yes, but I didn't know what I was looking at in there. You'll have to wait until you feel better to take a look."

I glance over his shoulder and see Margaret standing on the back porch, holding a broom in the air, and swinging it down as she mouths loudly, "Knock him on the head."

I make sure to keep myself between Archie and Margaret as we leave. "Come on. Let's go get those stitches fixed. And maybe we should use the yard gate while we're at it."

Chapter Seven

Dr. Sharpe is not impressed that we're back.

"I thought you were the ER doctor."

"Urgent care and ER are connected in this tiny hospital. The only difference is the cost of the bill."

"Not thrilled with small-town life?"

He keeps his eyes focused on Archie's face. "I forgot that quaint and broke sit next to each other at the table of life."

I nod, and Archie's eyes shoot back and forth between the doctor and me. He's always been the jealous sort. Interestingly, it was a quality I loved about him when we were married. I'd always wanted a man who wanted me all to himself. Archie was that...until he walked away.

Dr. Sharpe finishes the stitches. He catches my eye, then says, "There. Now, no more strenuous *anything*."

"Anything?" Archie asks slyly while looking at me with raised eyebrows.

"Anything," the doctor replies firmly.

"What about—"

"He said *anything!*" I snap, knowing that the doctor is giving me an out.

He's the one who put me in this spot. At least he's giving me an excuse to keep Archie out of my bed.

With a final lecture, Archie is released with strict instructions to avoid any physical strain. We drive home and stop for doughnuts at the drive-through. If there is a day that calls for doughnuts, this is it. Archie sits in the passenger seat, glancing through his satchel.

"Oh, I have the avocado." He smiles warmly at me. "I'll have to think of where to put it next. You know it will be a good one. Hopefully, I'll remember where I actually put it," he says with a laugh.

"Too soon, Archie. Too soon."

The avocado keychain is something that started when we were engaged. We got it at a fair and spent way too much money on it. We began trading it back and forth, hiding it in unique places. Sometimes, it would take the other person a couple of weeks to find. The whole point of the avocado, though, was to remember a fun time and to remember that the other person was always thinking of them. It was so that we wouldn't forget our first love. If anyone had to go out of town, we could count on the other one to hide the avocado in the bag or in the car or some other surprising place. The avocado didn't change hands very often in the last year of our marriage.

Our love had died, and the avocado is an example of it. I haven't seen it in a year. So, to see it in his satchel when I'd climbed into the plane was enough to give me pause. To hear him joking about it chips away at my heart even more—something I didn't know was possible.

"Speaking of forgetting things...I'm assuming my car is at the airport."

Fib, Meyer. You can do this. One small fib to get him healed. "Actually you drove down to Arizona and flew back."

Archie shrugs as though I didn't just lie to his face and continues searching through the satchel. "I don't remember this iPad. I must've bought this recently."

"Yes," I say, trying to not give anything away. Multiple lies will get me into trouble.

"I quit my job. What do I do now?"

"You eat doughnuts," I tell him as I take the box from the woman at the window.

Passing it to him, I lean forward and stuff some money in the tip jar, then drive toward home. I hold my hand out and wait for him to set a glazed doughnut in my hand.

"What am I supposed to do with myself while I heal?"

"Binge-watch all your favorite shows. Take naps. Go eat more doughnuts. Call your mom."

I need to call her first, though, because she's avoiding my calls. She was *not* in my driveway like I'd expected her to be this morning, and I think she's ghosting me.

"Actually, that's a really good idea. You should call your mom. Because she's probably very worried about you." I shove the doughnut in my mouth. Glazed ones are practically collapsible.

Archie clears his throat. "Oh, I talked to her this morning."

That is news to me. "Is she coming to get you?"

He shifts so he can face me while eats his own doughnut.

"Why would she come get me?"

I wiggle uncomfortably, realizing that his mother did not say anything concrete to him about coming to get him. Holly and I are going to have a heart-to-heart when I get ahold of her.

"I just think that your mom would be able to help you heal faster."

The car is quiet until I pull into the driveway.

"We had a doozy of a fight, didn't we?" he asks quietly.

I nod slowly.

"On a scale of one to ten, where are we?"

"Eleven," I say without hesitation.

"That's bad."

There's no sense in denying the truth, so I nod again. Just call me a bobblehead.

He reaches a hand over to grasp mine. He squeezes gently. "I'm sorry you're in this position. It's not fair to you, especially when I don't even remember what we fought about. If you need some time, then I can go stay with my mom. I know she wouldn't mind."

I'm not sure I agree with him on that, given that his mother is avoiding coming to get him, but I have a feeling it is because she is hoping some miracle will happen, like we will reconcile.

But Archie offering this? It's the perfect excuse to send him back.

"I really appreciate that, Archie. I think it might be best for you to stay with your mom. That way I won't mess up and say something I shouldn't." I turn my hand in his and squeeze back. Because it is considerate of him. "Let's take it one day at a time and see if we can get ahold of your mom."

"Would it help if I went and got a hotel in town?"

I rest my hand on the door handle. "I don't think it'd be good for you to be by yourself after such a major head injury. I would worry too much. You might as well stay here at the house."

Archie nods. "Well, I'd like to help you. I'm so glad you're doing your button earring business. Is there something I can help you with there? Do you need anything drawn?"

Where was this support a year ago? When he wanted me to be successful at a real estate career? To be some big shot? Instead of letting my biting questions fly, I pop open the door. Gatsby is sitting on the front porch, meowing at me.

"I'm sure I have something you could help with."

He smiles slowly at that. "That sounds great."

I spend the rest of the afternoon in my little workroom, making earrings. When I step out into the living room, I find Archie sitting, hunched over the coffee table, drawings scattered around him. They're beautiful, of course. The man is only capable of creating something gorgeous. He can fill a restaurant napkin with a perfect portrait.

People have begged for his doodles to take to their tattoo artists. Whatever he makes is full of his creative mind. He feels the world with everything in him. And then he lets his hand be the conduit through which he shares what he sees.

One of the doodles jumps out at me. Buttons scattered across the page, interwoven with thorny roses.

Other sketches include portraits of me wearing the button earrings. Some of them are of an imaginary child, wearing the kids earrings I make. He created a cartoon drawing of me stooped over a work desk. Gatsby is even there, perched on the edge of the table, batting his toy mouse back and forth. I can't see what Archie's working on right now, but curiosity has a firm grip on me.

I watch him for a moment while he's intent on his work. The music playing through the Bluetooth speaker next to him matches the timing of his pen strokes.

He finally sits back, and I catch my breath.

It has nothing to do with M's Buttons. And everything to do with us.

It's a drawing of me standing at the fair, holding that stinkin' avocado key chain.

There's a lightness in my eyes that I'm not sure I'll ever see again, an excited tilt of my lips as I look up at something. And though he's not on the page, I know exactly what I was looking at—him.

Some things never change.

"Oh, hey! I didn't hear you come in. I hope you don't mind. I needed something to do. There's something here. There's something in the drawing. I feel like I can almost remember, especially when I was drawing this of you."

He gestures to the picture that held my attention. "The memories...they're right there."

"Do you remember that day?"

"Vividly. It's the other memories that are circling it." He looks up, his eyes glassy. "If we're on a scale of eleven out of ten, our fight was big."

"Colossal."

"I hurt you." He runs a hand through his hair. "It's like I can feel a memory hovering. I can almost taste it. The anger. What happened?"

"We hurt each other," I reply. Probably the most honest thing I've said to myself, even.

"We fought about this couch." He pats the robin-egg-blue couch his fine ass is sitting on.

I freeze, watching his fingers caress the fabric. "You remember."

"Not everything. It's just this hovering thing. I remember being upset about this couch," he admits. "I must have thought it was uncomfortable."

I take a deep breath. He may remember that we fought about this couch, but he doesn't remember that I bought it *after* he left me.

"Have we talked about forgiving each other yet?" he continues as though we're discussing where we should go for dinner.

"No," I manage to say.

"We didn't—that is—" He clears his throat. "We didn't cheat, did we?"

"No!" I reply firmly.

One of our conversations as a young married couple was that cheating was never an option. There was nothing either of us could imagine being so hurtful. We promised that if we ever reached that point, we would tell the other one first, then go our separate ways. But there would be no secret feelings, no secret longings that would sneak out to hurt the other person. If we felt those things, we were honor-bound to tell the other person that it was the end of our relationship.

He rubs his pencil between his hands, as though he were trying to start a fire. "It's almost there. I can feel it. But it makes my head hurt."

I want him to push. I want him to remember. I want him to hurt again. Because I know I'm about to shatter.

I take a slow, deep breath and push down the rage. The rational part of my brain reminds me that my hands aren't clean in the event of our divorce. But the part of my brain that's trying to fake it with my ex-husband is screaming at me to tell him the truth; consequences be damned.

I lick my lips and say, "It's Kingston's birthday tonight. Do you want to stay here and rest?"

He looks at me with big puppy-dog eyes.

"Or would you like to come with me?"

He's already stacking his papers. "Sounds great! Are we going to Rye Brews?"

"Yes."

We always go to Rye Brews for Kingston's birthday. It's where you go for any birthday. It's a good restaurant, and in the evening, it transforms itself into a honky-tonk bar, complete with dancing. Kingston happens to be a dancing fool, so it's standard to show up there. Unfortunately, his birthday night doesn't line up with the line-dancing night, where he gets especially rowdy.

"What did we get him for his birthday?"

"I'm still deciding."

My brother is the gift giver, and it's really hard to come up with a good gift for the guy who is the best gift giver.

"I was thinking about getting him a membership to the country club."

"He'll love that. Okay, do I have any clean pants I can wear tonight?"

Annnd that was classic Archie.

"Depends, did you wash any?"

Classic Archie, meet New Meyer.

Chapter Eight

"Hello?"

Usually, I only answer calls for Willa or family. Phone calls are never good. The last time I answered an unknown number, I brought home an ex-husband.

Luckily, it's Willa calling right now.

"Guess what!" Willa's bright tone filters through.

"You booked us a promotional deal in Palm Springs?"

She laughs. "No, but it's just as good. They emailed the rough terms of the contract, and I'm in the negotiation phase!"

"They?"

"Blanchett!" Something similar to a high-pitched squeal hits my ears. "Can you believe it? They want you to be ready for a fall line!"

The blood rushes in my ears, and I wonder if I'm about to turn into a swooning regency heroine. *Contract* is a painfully official term. Not one I want in my vocabulary. But it is the next step to growing my business. It's the natural progression of things.

"I don't know that I would have gone to such lengths for anyone but you. I'm so happy to see you succeed."

Any protest at signing the contract dies on my lips.

"That's so sweet of you," I manage to say.

A shadow and a creak by the door tell me that Archie is coming. He raps on the doorframe but stops when he sees me on the phone.

I wave him in as I try to focus on the details that Willa is telling me. Production times, percentage of profits, launch dates, et cetera. There are so many numbers and excitement levels being thrown out that I can't keep track of it all.

Archie slowly wanders around the office, taking in every detail. I know he's trying to stir his memories, but this won't do it. I completely transformed this room when he left. What was first a hobby/guest room is now strictly a workroom.

I sold the guest bed on social media and then bought some secondhand shelves. I spruced them up with a couple layers of paint, and the shelves now organize my buttons and packaging systems.

He touches the buttons in the trays and picks up an etched wooden one to examine.

"So, I'll get back to him and see if I can hammer out those last few details in the contract before he sends an official one for us to sign," Willa says.

Archie turns to me as he holds up a white button to his ear and raises his eyebrows.

I give him a thumbs-up as I say good-bye to Willa.

"You look shocked," he says as he puts the button away.

"I feel shocked." I set my phone on the tabletop with a click. It sounds more like Judge Judy's gavel in the quiet room.

Archie slides a stool over to my worktable and sits down. He leans his elbows on the tabletop and rests his face in his hands. He's purposely trying to look silly, and it makes me smile.

"Tell me all about it. I've got all the time in the world. In fact, I have two extra years."

I snort, trying not laugh like I've lost my mind. "Willa, my PR manager, landed me a contract with Blanchett."

Archie's ridiculous face morphs into incredulous. "Meyer, that's amazing! So, that means that you'll be selling your earrings through a big-box store?"

I nod weakly.

"That's a big deal! We should celebrate it!" He stands up from the stool and heads toward the door. "This calls for dessert." He pauses when he turns back to me. "You don't seem exceptionally thrilled."

"I'm still shocked." Which is true. I don't know how I feel about it. Am I hesitant because it's something I don't want? Or am I hesitant because it's all so new?

"You need time to process. Want to go for a walk? Take a nap? Eat a doughnut? Make a doughnut?" His look turns decidedly not innocent. "You know what always helps me..."

I jump up. "A walk is a great idea! Brilliant." Because if I pick nap, he might try to nap with me. Any other option involves time spent with Archie.

"I'll come with you."

"You're still limping."

"Barely. It's just a bruise that hurts."

"No. You stay here and rest up."

I step out of the office and shut the door, effectively leaving my decision locked in that room.

◉

The brisk walk that bordered on a snail's-pace jog was exactly what I needed. Did it help me with the big decision? No. No, it did not. But it did stop me from packing my bags and fleeing to a country where I didn't speak the language.

I'm in a calmer frame of mind and ready for the evening—mostly.

It scares me to take Archie out in public in such a small town, but I group-texted everyone, and they're in on the details. A lot of shocked emojis were sent back, but ultimately, they agreed to try and not say anything that would mess with Archie's memories.

"Why do I have a garment bag?" Archie yells from the guest room.

"Because you gave up your slogan T-shirts!" I call back as I slip on a pair of white button earrings.

"When did I begin wearing jackets?"

"A year ago!" I mumble as I try to do my mascara without smudging it.

"Am I a classy guy or what?"

"Or what!" I yell back as I uncap my lipstick.

"I heard that!" he shouts back.

I laugh and smudge my lipstick. "You smeared my lipstick!"

The bathroom door wrenches open, and Archie is standing there, looking like a snack in a suit jacket and tie with jeans. He looks good.

"Come here. I'll show you smeared lipstick."

He advances on me with a predatory grin, and I squeak as I back up against the countertop. I hold the lipstick tube between us in self-defense.

"Now, Archie!" I manage to get out.

"Now? Well, if you insist." He's getting closer, crowding my space. He reaches his left hand up to the knot on his tie. I freeze momentarily. His wedding band is still on.

All this time and it hasn't crossed my mind that he's still wearing the simple gold band.

I assumed he had hurled it from the highest bridge in Arizona.

But right now, that ring is flashing as he tries to loosen his tie. He didn't throw it away.

"No! We'll be late! We definitely don't have time for that."

He rolls his eyes like an aggrieved middle schooler. "I was afraid you'd say that."

"We don't want to be late for dinner."

Archie's shoulders sag in defeat. "Fine. We'll be on time, then. How do I look?"

I study him and offer one simple word. "Amazing."

His Adam's apple bobs up and down as he watches me. My voice came across as huskier than usual.

Not good, Meyer. Danger zone ahead.

He starts to bend his head down. "Let's be late."

"Archie!" I bite out. "You need to recover. I've seen you limping around this house, and I notice you're actually taking the prescription-strength Tylenol, which means your headaches aren't gone. You need to take the time to heal. Doctor's orders."

"I've decided I don't like that guy." With a heavy sigh, he steps back to the door, providing a safer distance between us. "Fine. But if you were wondering, my stitches feel much better." He winks at me. "Once they've dissolved, I'll be good to go."

"Go where? Back to work?"

His deep chuckle echoes loudly as he leaves the room.

I dig through the drawer and pull out the deodorant. I'm going to need another layer. This bathroom is exceptionally warm this evening.

Chapter Nine

Archie holds the door open for me as I step into Rye Brews, the only bar and grill in town.

I spot Bailey immediately because she's already on the dance floor with her husband, Dan. God bless them; they're horrible at dancing. But they always have the most fun. Archie chuckles when he glimpses them.

"They're at it again." His shoulder bumps against mine as he says, "Do you think they'll have another baby in nine months?" He waggles his brows.

I can't stop the smile that creeps up my face. "Leo would be horrified. I think he likes being the youngest."

"I think that means he needs a younger sibling," Archie replies.

I turn to look around the room and find our table of friends.

Kingston isn't here yet—something I'm grateful for. He's the only one who didn't reply to the group text. I just hope he received the text that I'd sent.

Was it the coward's way out? Yes, which is why I chose it.

I texted Mom and Dad earlier today, and they support my decision to protect Archie until Holly can come get him. They've always liked Archie as well, and they were sad when things didn't work out for us. Although they were upset when Archie walked away, they still wished the best for him.

Kingston? Not so much. He took personal offense at the desertion of his sister. Although, I've often wondered if it had more to do with him feeling deserted by his friend.

"Hey, Archie!" Rylan jumps up from the table and pulls Archie into one of those awkward man-hug things, complete with a back slap. He greets me with a side hug and a whispered question. "Has he remembered yet?"

"No," I whisper back.

I wait for Archie to slide into the booth first. I always have to go to the bathroom a million times. No one wants me to be on the inside of a booth seat—not unless they're hoping they can get some extra exercise.

Rylan's wife, Kay, smiles and greets us. I've been getting to know her more over the recent months. At first, I wasn't sure I liked her. Then, I discovered she is more introverted than me. The reason she'd even gotten to know Rylan well enough to marry him was because the man doesn't recognize barriers—of any kind. It's his best and worst trait. *Everyone* is Rylan's best friend. So much so that you are never quite sure what he actually thinks about people. One guy can't love hanging out with that many people, can he?

But I guess that is why he does so well owning a restaurant and bar. Rye Brews is his baby, and he does really well with it.

It makes me tired, watching him socialize.

But Archie and Rylan hit it off—nothing new where Rylan is concerned—but Archie was picky about his friends, so it was a big deal for him to get along with Rylan.

Most of his guy friends were a result of hanging out with family or with my friends' husbands.

In his words, he didn't like to bother with fake friendships.

"Sit down and tell us all about it, man!" Rylan's loud voice sounds as if Archie's never been gone.

Come to think of it, I don't know if he kept speaking to Archie after he left or not. Mainly everyone avoided the awkward conversation of my ex-husband with me. I assumed that Rylan still talked with Archie some, even with states between them.

I swore him to secrecy about *the incident*, and now, I'm worried if he kept that promise or not.

"So, how much do you remember?" Rylan asks as he settles into a chair next to his wife.

Jack and Lira walk up and sit down at the table, greeting Archie as well. I went to high school with Lira, and we've somehow managed to stay in touch over the years. She married her high-school sweetheart who recently retired from the military.

Archie reaches for the brew list sitting on the table and tips it up to whisper loudly at me. "I remember Jack and Lira are engaged, right?"

Lira laughs, having overheard him. "Married now! And pregnant!"

"What?" Archie and I exclaim together. He drops the brew list on the table. We're all surprised by that one.

"You didn't say anything!" I finally say.

Multiple voices tumble over each other, offering their congratulations.

Lira waves a hand through the air. "You know I don't have enough time for that big announcement stuff."

I'm genuinely happy for them.

Lira is glowing, and Jack has a *cat-that-ate-the-canary* grin plastered on his face. If their level of excitement is any indicator, they'll make excellent parents.

We fall into easy conversation, joking about the lack of a birthday boy, then small talk. Everyone is careful to keep it light, never touching on anything that will trigger Archie's memories.

Just when I start to relax and think that the evening is going to end without incident, I spot disaster on the horizon. *Hard-a-port.* Time to turn this ship around. This is not going to end well.

Willa is walking toward us purposefully. Not that it's different from her usual walk. She probably walks the same way when she's heading to bed. But that's not what makes me want to crawl under the table and hide among the spilled beer on the floor.

Nope.

It's the man she's pulling behind her. She showed me his picture a couple weeks ago, telling me she had a good friend she wanted to set me up with. I was noncommittal about the whole thing.

This is him.

I turn to look at Archie, who's sitting next to Dan, talking with him. Bailey is still in the restroom, which means I need to ward off Willa first.

I start to get up when Archie reaches over and grasps my hand.

"Meyer, what was the name of that art gallery we went to on our honeymoon? I was thinking of that giraffe painting for Lira's baby."

My heart stutters as I see Willa and her friend rapidly approaching the table. The new baby, while exciting, is months down the road. This impending disaster is only mere seconds away.

"Seaboard Art."

"Oh yeah, thanks." He squeezes my hand and turns back to Dan.

I turn to get up, but Willa is standing right next to me, smiling down at me.

"Meyer! I'm so glad we ran into you here! I wanted to introduce you to my friend I was telling you about!"

I cough and try to pull my hand from Archie's.

He lets go and begins patting my back. "Are you okay?"

"Fine, great." I keep coughing and wonder if I can keep it up long enough that Willa will give up and walk away.

"I know the Heimlich. Do you want me to help you?" Willa asks oh-so helpfully.

"No, that's okay." I flinch as she rests a hand on my shoulder, and I wait for her to start pounding on my back. The fear makes me able to stop coughing.

"This is my friend Brent."

Archie leans closer to me and slips an arm around my shoulders, pulling me against his side. "Are you going to introduce me?" he murmurs to me, but it's loud enough for both Willa and Brent to hear.

Willa's eyes widen, and she glances frantically between us. I move my face in a mix of strange contortions.

"Willa!" I finally manage. "You remember Archie?"

Willa tips her head to the side and studies Archie. "*Archie*, Archie?" Her words are slow and deliberate.

"Yes. *Archie*, Archie." Hopefully, my facial expressions aren't a mirror of hers.

"Okaaay. Yes. *Archie*, Archie. Well...wow. I, um, wanted to introduce you to Brent..." She leans over and grasps his hand in hers. The surprised look on his handsome face shows me this isn't a regular move between friends. "...so that we could all get to know each other better. You know, with me talking about him all the time and stuff."

She pats a hand against his chest awkwardly. And now, Brent looks mildly amused.

"Well, we don't want to hold you up. It was nice meeting you, Archie!"

Archie waves as they walk away.

"Who is that?" Archie whispers.

"She handles my marketing."

"What? You have your own PR lady?"

"Yes. Remember I told you about her already? Oh, but I forgot the doctor said there might be some blank spots as you're healing."

"I'm so proud of you, Meyer," Archie says sincerely, and it makes me want to cry.

"Thank you. I need to run to ask her about a project real quick, if you're okay here."

"I'm fine." His fingers brush against mine as I stand from the booth.

I need to catch her and explain about Archie before she says something to the wrong person.

"Willa," I whisper her name loudly as I walk toward her and Brent.

"What?"

"Don't you need to use the restroom, too?" I ask with a tense smile as Brent's head ping-pongs between us.

"Oh, yes!" Willa exclaims. "I definitely do. Let's go together."

We head toward the back of the bar and down a short and narrow hallway that doesn't leave room for a large dog, but at least it hides us from view.

"Willa, that's my husband out there. I was so distracted the last few times we spoke that I haven't said anything."

"Husband? Don't you mean, ex-husband?"

I wave a hand through the air and brush my bangs back into place. "Yes."

She shakes her head. "I didn't even know you were talking to him again! And you're here with him?!"

"More like he's here with me. He has amnesia, and he thinks we're still married."

Willa looks at me as though I were the one with amnesia. Then, she laughs lightly. "What did you say when you told him?"

I puff out my cheeks and blow out a long breath.

"Ohhh, I see. You haven't told him."

I shake my head. "The doctor thought it would be better for him to learn about it in his own time and that the memories would eventually come back."

"Oh girl...you're in a bit of a mess, aren't you?" Willa asks as she helps straighten my hair.

"A colossal mess," I agree.

By the time I return to the table, Kingston is sitting in a chair across from Archie. He's looking a little too serious for the birthday boy, but he still stands up to wrap me in a bear hug. My brother and I look similar. His hair is only a few shades lighter than mine, although he's several inches taller and believes in strength training. Sometimes it feels like hugging a steel post.

"Happy birthday, you big baby."

"Careful, tiny. You're next," he replies as he tweaks my hair.

"Any dying requests?"

"Was that Willa I saw you with?" he asks, ignoring my teasing question.

"Yes." I refuse to be the pawn in his revolving game of love—or lust, more like.

"Why don't you invite her over here?" He's still staring after her.

"Because she's here on a date."

Kingston mutters something under his breath that I can't hear. I shrug it off and wish him a happy birthday. I pull the card out of my purse and pass it across the table to him.

"The big twenty-nine." I smirk. "You're almost middle-aged."

"Oh, hush up, pipsqueak," he replies fondly. He unceremoniously rips the card open and quickly reads the words in it.

"It says *get well soon*." He mock frowns at me.

I catch Archie hiding a grin behind his hand.

"Well, I thought you could do better..."

It's been a running joke between Kingston and me over the years to always get a completely unrelated card for each other's major events. He gave me an *I'm-sorry-for-your-loss* card at my high school graduation.

I gave him a *congratulations-on-the-new-baby* one at his college graduation. His girlfriend at the time didn't appreciate my humor—at all.

"You bought me a membership to the country club?" The excited note in his voice tells me I did well.

"With my long-standing membership there, it wasn't difficult."

The entire table laughs at my quip.

Me joining any kind of club that requires frequent socialization would be my version of sending an SOS to the universe. *Help! Aliens have overtaken my brain!*

"Thanks for this, sis." He stands up and leans across the table to awkwardly hug me.

The beer glasses teeter, but then it's finally my water glass that loses it and floods the table. Water isn't a hugger.

"Dang, sorry about that," Kingston mutters as he pulls back.

Archie jumps into action, mopping up the water with a few stray napkins. He finds one more and reaches over to dry the wet patch on my jeans.

I'm painfully aware of both his hands, one frantically dabbing and the other bracing just above my knee, as though I'm going to somehow get away in this tight booth.

"Why are you drinking water tonight?" Archie asks.

The jokes about Kingston spilling the cup cut off abruptly.

"Oh, you know." I laugh weakly.

"You always get a margarita here. I've never once seen you drink water."

My cheeks are flaming.

"Oh. Are we pregnant?"

The complete look of shock on his face has me blurting out the truth before he goes into cardiac arrest.

"I'm sober now! You just don't remember." I smile softly, hoping that will make everything better.

"As if him remembering would make anything better," Kingston mumbles from across the table.

I give him a swift kick to the shin underneath the table.

"What does he mean?" Archie asks me, but he's busy having a glaring contest with my brother.

"It's because of you," Kingston replies.

"What?"

"You can't be serious, Meyer," Kingston snaps his glare over to me. "You can't *not* tell him everything. He deserves to know."

"Know what?"

"That your wife had to take care of her own problems. You're the reason she doesn't drink anymore."

Kingston has a dark look in his eye that I know only prophesies bad things to come. If he spills out the truth, happy Archie will be destroyed.

Chapter Ten

"Archie, I think it's time to go home," I say as I glare at my brother.

Archie's eyes are ping-ponging around the table as he tries to figure out what is going on. But I need to get him out of here before my brother starts a fight with him.

A physical fight, that is. He's already been trying to instigate a verbal one. Archie just doesn't know it.

I grab my purse from where it's sandwiched between Archie and me, then slide out of the booth, my knee bumping against Rylan's in my hurry to get out. I nearly stumble forward, but Archie catches me from behind, helping me regain my balance.

He senses my urgency or possibly has questions of his own. His hand steadies me, and I'm back on sure footing in no time at all. He propels me toward the door with a firm hand on my elbow. I'm not sure if he's rescuing me or leading me to my doom.

Neither of us bothers to say goodbye to the rest of the group.

No words are spoken as we walk to the car. A misting rain dampens my bangs enough that they stick to my forehead.

We climb into the car, and when I start it, I have to turn the defrost on to fight the instant fog of a warm car against the rain.

The streetlamp above my parking spot glares off the hood of the car, even brighter with the drops of rain puddling together.

Archie leans over and flicks on the radio. He scrolls through stations—country, classic, rock—then settles on a mournful tune being crooned on the oldies station. "Moon River" by Andy Williams.

I fold my arms together and rest my forehead against the steering wheel as my arms shake.

Archie reaches over to rub gentle circles on my back.

I can't hold in the laugh that bubbles out.

"Only you would walk away from someone spoiling for a fight and turn on 'Moon River' to make me feel better." I turn my head to the side so I can smile up at him.

"You're laughing, though, aren't you? So, my method must be working."

Straightening, I smile once more. "It's not failing. Let's go home."

He turns the volume up and begins belting out the lyrics. His innate ability to remember every song lyric there ever was, always made me a tad jealous. But it also came in handy when he was trying to cheer me up. He could even do impressionist singing, which was some-thing that would guarantee we were in a good mood.

The song ends, and he turns the volume down. We watch the windshield wipers try to keep up as we drive through the ever-thickening rain.

"You gave up drinking?" he finally asks.

I nod slowly. "I realized it was getting out of hand."

"But you don't drink very much."

Two years ago, he would have been right. But that wasn't the case for post-divorce, self-medicating Meyer.

"I was starting to use it as a way to numb. And then there was a moment where it got me into trouble, and I knew I needed to stop."

Archie's tongue circles his lips before he says, "Do you want me to quit with you? Because I will if that will help you."

I jerk the wheel when I realize I was paying closer attention to Archie's mouth than pulling into my driveway.

After narrowly missing the mailbox, I park the car in front of the garage. The rain is pouring down now, and I realize I haven't answered his question.

"That's okay, Archie. I actually feel better not drinking, and if I don't start again, then I'll be fine. I quit before it got to the addiction level. I just never want to risk that being me."

We sit and stare at the house together. Gatsby is standing at the living room window, batting at raindrops as they slide down the window.

"What did Kingston mean when he said it was my fault?"

I roll my shoulders as I try my best to formulate an answer—an answer that won't give everything away.

"First of all, this was not your fault. You didn't make these choices. I did. You were in Arizona at the time, wor—er, visiting your mom. I drank too much at the bar one night. A guy came on to me. I thought I had made it clear I wasn't interested." I tap my fingers against the steering wheel and take a few short breaths. "He wouldn't take no for an answer."

Archie's sharp intake of breath nearly has me turning to look at him. But I can't. Not if I am going to tell him this. And for some reason, I know I need to. I haven't told the details to anyone. No one knows how scared I was. No one knows how I begged him to let me go.

"He came up behind me while I was opening my purse. Grabbed my hair and shoved me against the car. Told me he knew I wanted it." My voice shakes, and I hate that I still can't control the tremor of fear through me.

The rain is lessening, but we remain frozen there.

"I pushed back, and I guess he wasn't expecting it because I knocked us off balance. I fell to the ground." I absentmindedly rub my elbow where I still have a scar from the pavement. "Luckily, my purse had spilled everywhere, and my keys had fallen close to me. I hit the panic button on the key fob. He reached for me again, and I tried kicking him, but everything was so slow. I'd drunk too much. My reactions were slow."

Now, it's my tears blurring my vision rather than the rain.

"Rylan came running out of the bar. He said he heard the car alarm and my scream. Rye started yelling and running for us. The guy let go and ran off."

My body is shaking as I finish the story, and I have to take a minute before I can turn to face Archie.

His cheeks are red, and his brow is furrowed. His lips are set in an angry, hard line. "I'm going to kill him. Or did I already?"

That startles a short laugh out of me because it's what I needed to hear. No accusations for what I could have done better in that situation. Just pure, unadulterated support and protection.

"Where is he?" Archie asks.

"In the state penitentiary. Apparently, he had an arrest warrant and a long enough rap sheet to be put away for years."

"Good. Now, come here."

Before I can explain it to myself, I find myself climbing over the middle console of the car with the intention of curling up on Archie's lap.

My butt bumps against the horn, startling me. I try to shift away, but then I accidentally plant a sharp elbow against Archie's chest.

"Ouch."

Now, my foot is caught in the seatbelt, and I can't move.

"Hold still," Archie says.

Ha. So much for a smooth hug. Now, I'd like to crawl into a puddle of embarrassment, please.

He leans forward to untangle the seatbelt from my foot. I'm bent down with my face pressed against his thigh as we try to untangle the mess I'm in.

"Got it." He places his large hands on my hips and lifts me onto his lap. Superhuman strength for Archie.

He must have started lifting weights in the time that he's been gone.

He wraps his arms around me and tugs me close.

I lay my head against his chest.

"I wasn't there for this?"

"No," I whisper. "We were both being dumb and fighting. Part of the reason for your visit to Arizona."

He presses a gentle kiss to my forehead and trails a hand through my hair. "I'm sorry. So very sorry that I wasn't there when you needed me."

"Sometimes, life happens that way. You can't always stop things from happening. Everyone has apologized to me. Rylan apologized, as though it were his fault because it was his bar. The police officer apologized. Kay apologized. Kingston kept saying he should have been there with me. And I finally realized that, while they were all well intentioned and loving me by saying this, I knew I needed to learn how to be there for myself. And it's ended up being okay. I've become stronger because of it. I've taken self-defense classes. I'm prepared for it. I know what to do. And do you know what? I no longer walk through the parking lot in fear. How strange is that? I was more afraid before that happened than after."

Archie squeezes me tight against his chest again. This time, I'm not sure I'll be able to breathe, but then he releases his hold on me, and I realize I'm not shaking anymore.

"You know I absolutely hate that this happened to you and that I don't remember any of it. But I'm so glad you feel better about yourself. You're a strong woman, and I don't want you to ever doubt that."

This strong woman is in serious danger of having her heart melted by her ex-husband.

But I don't say that. "Thank you, Archie."

He sighs. "Come on. I'm too old to sit in a car. Let's go inside."

He pops open the door, and I prepare to climb out, but he keeps a tight hold on me as he stands up. There's a slight wobble as he bumps back into the car, but I cling to his neck, like that will keep us upright.

It must work because he regains his balance, manages to shut the door, and carries me up to the house.

"You're going to pull your stitches," I remind him.

"Hush," he says as he steps onto the small porch. "Door's locked."

Archie mutters under his breath, then asks, "Do you have the keys?"

"No, they're in the car." I laugh.

He groans, then says, "Don't go away."

He sets me down and jogs back to the car through the now-heavy rain, grabs the keys and my purse, then comes back to unlock and open the door. He tosses my purse carelessly inside, then turns around, scooping me off my feet.

He kicks the door closed, but it doesn't latch all the way. He growls—yes, freaking growls—at the door, then shoves it closed with his good shoulder. Carrying me to the bedroom, he sets me on the bed and pulls the shoes from my feet. He tugs the covers out from under me, then pushes me to the center of the bed.

"I haven't showered yet," I whisper.

"Stop being practical," he whispers back as he boops my nose. "I just want to tuck you in tonight. Okay?"

I stare at him and realize he needs this. He needs to see me tucked safely in bed. And while it might be a year too late, I want it as much as he needs it.

He tucks the covers in all the way to my shoulders, then leans down to kiss my forehead. "I love you, Meyer Dunmore. And I'm so glad you're my wife."

But I'm not.

Chapter Eleven

Despite my plan to climb out of bed and take a shower the second Archie left the room, I ended up falling fast asleep. I wake up in the same clothes I'd worn to the bar the night before. And now, I'll be washing my sheets today.

First thing, instead of showering, I go for a walk. Being outside always gives me fresh perspective on life, and perspective is something I need. Badly.

The lake is only half a mile from my house, and it's my favorite spot to hike. The trees surrounding the lake keep the traffic noise down, and it feels like you're the only person in the world.

If you go hiking on the weekend, it's completely different. That's why I know I'm completely spoiled to live so close. Avoiding the crowds is easy when it's convenient.

I can make it part of my morning routine—to get a brisk walk in. And I need a brisk walk today. I need to squash this blooming attachment, because Archie doesn't remember what I did.

His sweetness last night was because he didn't remember that I'd called him a self-absorbed artist. A cliché of his work.

I cringe as I step over a fallen log.

All this past year, I've been thinking of what *he* did wrong to *me*, desperate to hang on to my anger as I processed our separation. But now that I'm back around him, I'm starting to recall the things *I* said, the ways I hurt him.

When you see your own anger against the backdrop of someone else's love, it's easy to spot your shortcomings. And it's not pretty.

I stop in the middle of the small footbridge that crosses over a creek, which feeds into the lake.

The trickling of the water is unfortunate timing, as I recall that I drank a big bottle of water before I went on my hike. I'm still a mile from the nearest outhouse. Darn my problem-solving walk.

I can make it a long way in a short time. I break into a jog, but that just makes it worse. Then, I glide into a smooth, non-jolting walk. It's better, but it's still too slow.

I pass the fork in the trail and take the less-traveled road. I'm going to have to find a tree and practice my squatting. There's no other option besides peeing my pants.

Glancing around me several times, I hurry off the trail.

No one's around, so it should be fine. Right? I mean, I've had to pee outdoors before. It's not that big of a deal.

Is it terrifying? Yes. Is it exposing? Yes. A bear could just grab a quick little snack while I am busy peeing. Am I in dire straits? Yes. No more water before hikes. No more angry stomping. It seems to flush it out of your system faster.

I don't see any other hikers, so I dive behind a large huckleberry bush, picking my way around ferns and stinging nettle. *I'll make sure I don't sit on that.*

I keep going until I'm one hundred percent out of sight of the trail. I find a nice, big tree and check for poison oak, then scan up in the tree for a cougar, look behind me to make sure there're no bears, and then I take care of business.

Men are ridiculously lucky when it comes to peeing outside. It's crazy how easy it is for them. They can just carry on a conversation with you while they do it.

Oh yeah, did you see the score yesterday?

Look where the lightning struck that tree.

All while peeing.

They're hardly even exposed.

Women literally have their asses hanging out to do it.

My head is on a swivel, but when I'm finally done, I feel relief that I took the time to do this. Now, I don't have to frantically run or glide-walk to the rest stop.

As I start heading back to the trail, muted voices drift to me. They're male voices, and while last night I told Archie that I wasn't afraid anymore, I still have a certain sense of self-preservation, so I stay off the trail until their voices pass me by. It's better to hang out with the bears and cougars at this point. I have yet to be bitten or hurt by either one of those animals, whereas my heart has been broken by a man, and another man tried to break my body.

Bears seem downright friendly at this moment. I wait an extra full minute until the voices are long gone.

Finally, I step back onto the trail. I turn back and go toward the fork in the trail and head down a different route than before.

I glance at my watch, and I know I should be getting back to the house so I can start work, but that means I have to face Archie.

So, I jog a little. I don't want time to think.

I just need to feel the endorphins rushing through my body right now. I lose myself in my music. The sun is out, drying the trail that was soaked from the rain last night.

I dive off onto a trail that will loop back around to home faster. It's narrow and winding, and it circles to the trail that leads directly to my house. A connecting trail that comes down off the slope juts out to connect to the one I'm on. I catch a flash of movement on the other side of a large shrub.

Grabbing my keychain in my hand, I pick up my pace. As I'm passing the bush, a hand reaches out and grabs my shoulder.

I scream, "Fire!" as I spin around and spray my pepper spray blindly. I keep screaming, "Fire!" over and over, hoping to attract another Good Samaritan hiker. I tell myself I need to open my eyes.

I open them as the hand lets go of me, and two loud yells fill the air. I release my finger off the trigger, stop screaming, and pause my music.

"You scared me!" I accuse.

I take several large steps back from the floating fog of pepper spray.

Archie's already farther down the trail from me, and Dr. Tripp Sharpe is leaning against a tree trunk with his eyes pressed against the hem of his T-shirt. He's coughing loudly, and Archie is pulling a water bottle out of a small backpack.

I have so many questions.

"What are you doing here?"

Archie cracks open the water bottle and passes it to Tripp. "I was hoping I'd run into you on your hike this morning. Found Dr. Sharpe here instead. I saw you coming from the top of the hill and called out to you. Thought you heard me since you sped up."

Archie is grinning like a fool. And I have this overwhelming urge to smack that look right off his face. It's unfortunate none of the pepper spray hit his face.

"Why are you smiling? I just sprayed you both with pepper spray!"

Archie shakes his head. "You mostly got Dr. Sharpe since I was kind of the one holding your shoulder. I was more behind you than to the side. But I'm just so proud of you."

I shake my head slowly. I didn't know that having amnesia could make you lose your mind completely.

"Proud of me? He might never see again!"

Archie helps Dr. Sharpe rinse his eyes out with the clean water. "But you were ready. What you were saying last night wasn't just bragging. You did great protecting yourself! But what's the deal with yelling *fire*?"

Darn if he doesn't have the happiest look on his face.

And I feel an uncomfortable swelling in my chest at his approval. "No one wants to put themselves in harm's way with an attacker, but they might come check things out if there's a fire," I explain.

With a sigh, I tuck the pepper spray into the side pocket of my yoga pants. I walk closer to get a better look at Dr. Sharpe's face. He's blinking water out of his eyes as he turns to look at me.

"Are you all right?" I ask as I pat his shoulder. *Because that will make it better, Meyer.*

He manages a nod. "I got the edge of the mist. It's not too bad." His eyes are bright red, and the skin around them is flaming.

"Are you sure?"

He nods. "I've treated pepper-spray burns before. Trust me, if you get a full face of it, you know. It's powerful stuff, so I'm glad I wasn't standing too close."

"What are you doing here?" I ask.

"Someone told me that this was a great spot to hike. I thought I'd give it a try this morning, and I happened to run into Archie. We've been walking and talking a bit." He splashes a little more water onto his eyes. "Something that I'm regretting right now."

I make a sympathetic sound because, well, I should've at least had my eyes open before I pressed the pepper-spray button. Being prepared and paranoid are two different things.

"Can I help you get to the car? I could drive you back to your house." I hold onto his elbow.

Archie clears his throat. I turn and look at him, and he's rolling his eyes.

"His legs aren't broken," he snaps.

I nearly forgot about Jealous Archie. I *don't* let go of Dr. Sharpe's arm.

"Come on, you poor thing." I raise my eyebrows at Archie as he squints at me.

Archie falls into step next to me as I lead Dr. Sharpe down the trail.

Archie murmurs, "You never called me poor thing when I was in a plane wreck."

I narrow my eyes at him before I turn back to Dr. Sharpe. "You really should let me drive you home, poor guy."

"You're pushing it, Meyer," Archie whispers in my ear in a grim voice.

The hairs on the back of my neck stand up, and I shiver.

"What are you gonna do about it?" I reply with a tight smile.

He mumbles something that I can't understand. I'm not sure I want to know what he said.

I let go of Dr. Sharpe's arm, and we make it back to the main trailhead. "Next time you guys want to meet up with me for a hike, don't surprise me by jumping out from behind a bush and grabbing onto my shoulder."

Dr. Sharpe nods. "I think we've learned our lesson."

Archie has the decency to look embarrassed. "I should've known better than to grab your shoulder without making sure you heard me. I did call your name, but it must've been lost in the music."

"I know I shouldn't have been running with my music so loud. That doesn't keep me aware of my surroundings," I admit grudgingly. "And now, Dr. Sharpe has the worst of it."

Dr. Sharpe nods. "It was an accident all the way around. But I think, after this, you should probably just call me Tripp."

Archie glances at him out of the corner of his eye. "How does someone come to be named Tripp Sharpe anyway?"

Tripp shakes his head. "Easy. You have a trendy mother who gets remarried to a man who adopts you and gives you his last name."

"Rough."

Tripp smiles. "No, it's not too bad. My dad's a good guy, and I'm happy to have his last name."

"What's your dad do?"

Tripp smiles wryly, his red eyes watering. "He's a surgeon."

I bite my lip and try not to laugh. I bend my head down and see that Archie is fighting a smile too. I risk a glance at Tripp, but he has a full-blown grin on his face.

"It's okay. It's a family joke about the irony that Dad and I are both doctors with the last name of Sharpe."

Archie and I both smile at that.

"Do you know of any other good hikes around here?"

Archie pipes up and begins listing a number of hikes around the area. Soon, they're making plans to go on a hike together the next day, which is perfect for me. Gives Archie something to do, and I'm happy to see that he and the doctor are hitting it off.

I like Tripp. If it wasn't for Archie, I might even be attracted to Tripp. But I did have Archie—once upon a time. And he's thrown a wrench the size of Texas into every one of my plans.

"Do you know what Dr. Sharpe suggested?" Archie asks after I step out of the shower. His voice sounds through the door, but it's still too close for my tastes. He must be standing in the hallway.

I'm frightfully naked in here, and his voice is so very, very clear.

I frantically wrap myself in a towel and remind myself that proximity isn't the same as visibility. I grab a second towel a little more slowly and wrap my dripping hair in it.

"What did your new best friend say?" I tease because Archie switched from jealous husband to hiking enthusiast pretty quickly.

"That we should have a reminiscing night!"

I pull the towel a little tighter. "What does that mean?"

"He told me that, sometimes, talking about memories or looking at old pictures helps the more recent ones resurface! We could start with looking at our wedding pictures."

"When did the helpful doctor say all that?" I gripe as I towel-dry my hair.

"When I was talking to him in the parking lot."

I shake my head. It's like having a child. I can't leave him alone for a second because he'll be easily influenced by someone. I'm beginning to get annoyed my Dr. Helpful Tripp Sharpe. "I'll be out in a minute."

I pull on my jeans and a blouse and decide that my hair and makeup can wait until after I've had a cup of coffee. I pull open the bathroom door, only to find Archie standing in the hall.

I barely squeak my surprise. I'm stoic. I'm strong. Seeing Archie standing in the hall, holding our photo album, wearing an avocado T-shirt, doesn't surprise me. Not one bit.

"I think it's brilliant," Archie says as he reaches out and combs down my bangs in the direction that they should go.

Probably my not-so-wise choice post-divorce: bangs. Why, oh why, do women have the overwhelming urge to chop off chunks of our hair when we're under stress? I'll never know why, but I succumbed to the urge.

"Okay, that sounds great! Why don't you let me know how that goes?" I say as I hurry to the kitchen for that coffee.

"But he thought it would be a good idea for us to do it together."

"I have to make earrings this morning. And then go see Janice at the post office." I fill my mug with coffee. "I wish I could reminisce with you. It sounds fun." As fun as doing the dishes every day.

He's quiet for a blessed moment as I sip my coffee, regaining some life in my soul.

"Don't worry."

I immediately worry.

"I'll just tell you about the things I'm seeing!"

He grins, and much to my consternation, I can't come up with a good excuse. I needed this time to myself to be alone in blessed silence. Or listen to an audiobook. Something that didn't involve a walk down memory lane to remind me of everything I'd lost.

To avoid looking at our old wedding album, I pretend to be busy folding socks.

"Hey, did you smear cake on my face at the wedding? Because I seem to remember something...vaguely." Archie is leaning against the doorframe of my bedroom, a smirk on his face as he watches me fold socks. He's holding the wedding album open in one hand.

I reply primly, "You know very well that I tripped."

He flips the album toward me in one hand.

"Careful! You'll bend it." I gasp as I hurry to salvage the album.

Now I'm the one holding the album and staring at a picture of a ridiculously happy young couple.

Archie's face has a smear of frosting on it. There's a drop of frosting on my nose. And there's joy radiating off the page.

"I still don't believe you that it was an accident. Someday you'll admit it."

Not today, Satan.

Chapter Twelve

"Come on over for bocce night." Margaret's voice is loud, coming over the phone line. She still uses a landline rather than a cell phone. It seems to do something strange to the connection. Her voice is always much louder than anyone else's. And it has a bad echo, so her voice rings in my ears.

"Margaret, I'm not sure that's a good idea," I say.

Taking Archie out to socialize the last time ended in epic failure.

"It'll be fine. I'll make sure everyone is on their best behavior. We'll all pretend like we're living in the past— like someone else I know."

A sucker punch from a ninety-year-old. Just what I needed.

But Archie's questions are getting more pointed, and if he keeps going down this road, I'm going to have to tell him the truth. He deserves the truth if he's starting to piece it together himself. Although, I can't be sure it's because his memory is returning.

"Okay, we'll be there. What time?"

"Five-thirty. We're playing extreme tonight."

I groan, hopefully inwardly. Sometimes, Margaret has regular yard-game nights, where everyone plays croquet or badminton, like civilized people. Other times, she has nights where we play bocce extreme, which barely resembles the original game, besides using the same ball set.

"Sounds great." I don't mean that. "What are we doing for dinner?"

Game nights at Margaret's always entail a potluck dinner. But she makes sure there is a theme so we can plan our dishes accordingly. She once went on a curry kick, which I personally enjoyed, but she couldn't handle the spice.

"Hot dogs."

Well, that isn't very adventurous.

"I'll bring a salad."

I end the call and stare at the rows of black-and-white button earrings I've made. I've never had a simple color palette before.

I used to think it was boring.

Not anymore. Black and white is my new favorite. Simple. Safe. Peaceful. Everything I need in my life right now.

I find Archie in the backyard. The sun's out, and everything is drying up. The perfect pre-summer day. He's reading a book with Gatsby curled on his lap.

"It's bocce extreme tonight."

He looks up at me and nods slowly. "Good."

"I don't know if it's such a good idea for us to go."

"Why?"

I point at his head.

"It's fine. Nothing will happen to me."

"Maybe I should make you wear a helmet. Last time we played, you got hit in the head," I remind him, recalling the unfortunate moment his head started bleeding everywhere. The doctor had assured us it was normal for head wounds to gush. I didn't believe him.

He closes the book and turns to look at me. "I don't remember that."

Shoot. That happened more recently.

"Yeah, well, that's probably because it happened during the blank years. Margaret's throw went wide and caught you on the back of the head. It was a scary accident."

Archie looks amused. "Are we sure that's not what she's going to *try* to do tonight?"

I plant my hands on my hips. "You might be right. We're definitely not going. She's going to try and knock your memory back."

Archie laughs and stands up, forcing Gatsby to use his own feet to walk on. "Let's go. It sounds fun."

He picks the book up from the arm of the chair and steps toward me.

"What are you reading?" I turn my head sideways to try to catch the title. "*The Troubleshooting Guide to Cirrus SR20 Engines*. Wow. That looks like one I might want to borrow."

Archie frowns playfully and reaches up to touch a lock of my hair. "A guy tries to learn something, and you mock him."

"Me, mock you?" I ask in shock. I spin around to walk inside. "I would never mock you. I know your taxed mind couldn't take it."

A book smacks lightly against my ass as he follows me inside. "Keep it up, Meyer. Just keep it up and see."

"Come on. You can help me make a salad to take."

He slips a finger into the back pocket of my jeans as we walk into the kitchen. I reach back and smack his hand away.

"Quit that. You're far too intellectual for me."

The wicked gleam in his eye warns me I need to dodge out of his reach.

I jump toward the fridge, swinging the door open and spinning around. "Head! Salad! Leaf!"

"Bed," he fires back.

I stop. "What?"

He folds his arms across his chest as he studies me. "Oh, I thought we were throwing out random words."

I glare at him. "I'm trying to get you to keep your hands to yourself. That's what."

"You're no fun. We have time." He glances at the clock to corroborate his claim.

"We have to make the salad. And five-thirty isn't that far away." *And you don't remember anything yet.* Sleeping with Archie when he doesn't remember anything is one hundred percent wrong. Trying to stop him while preserving his fragile mental state may eventually break my mind.

"Yes, it is. Salad doesn't take that long to make."

"So much chopping. Here. Chop this." I reach

blindly behind me into the fridge and pass him a head of broccoli.

"You didn't even know what you were passing to me."

"Yes, I did. I was passing you something to keep your hands busy," I say with a cheeky grin.

He tweaks my nose and grabs the broccoli. "This means I will not be going easy on you tonight."

He marches to the cutting block. He pulls out a knife and is about to start chopping.

"Wait! Aren't you going to rinse that?" I ask as I start rinsing the lettuce.

"It's broccoli. It's fine." He raises the knife.

I throw the sponge at him and hit his arm, leaving a soapy square on his T-shirt sleeve.

He freezes. Then, he deliberately sets down the knife and stalks toward me, broccoli in hand.

My heart is in my throat, and I turn around to set the lettuce in the strainer before I make my quick getaway.

Too late.

He has me pinned in at the sink. His front is pressed against my back, and the countertop is digging against my hips.

"Here, why don't you help me?" his voice rumbles in my ear. And then he's holding the broccoli under the water, and his arms are acting as a cage.

I take a long, shaky breath as I try not to absorb every sensation.

"Oops," he says as he splashes a handful of water against my front.

I gasp at the cold and press back against him. He doesn't budge.

"I think the broccoli is rinsed now," I manage.

He splashes another handful of water against my front. This time, I *know* it wasn't an accident.

"Archibald Dunmore, you knock that off!"

"What are you talking about?" he asks in a fake inno-cent voice as he splashes me again.

"The broccoli is rinsed!" I practically shout.

"Oh no, you said I needed to rinse the broccoli, so I'm going to be extra thorough about it. Can't let any of those little germs sneak by."

Another splash. My shirt is white, and now, my front is completely soaked.

"I'm going to have to change before tonight, thanks to you." I can't even turn around to face him in the little space he's allowed me.

He bends down and sinks his teeth into my earlobe, his teeth clinking against my button earring. "We don't have to go."

I elbow him in the stomach and shut off the water. "Chop your broccoli!" I'm manic. Frantic. I've got to get out of his arms before I turn around and do something I'll regret...like kiss him.

He finally steps back and returns to the chopping block, a safe distance away.

"You look good in that shirt."

I shred the lettuce into the salad spinner. I smile at him sweetly. "I can't wait to play bocce extreme with you tonight."

Archie shudders. I might hate confrontation. I might hate voicing my opinion in any regular life, but throw me into a competition or game, and I turn into a completely different person. All bets are off.

Archie waves a stick of broccoli at me. "Play nice."

I'll play just as dirty as Archie has been.

❁

The yard is full. The hot dogs are being cooked on an outdoor grill. Bailey is chasing her kids away from the plane wreckage that still sits there as a tetanus hazard.

"At least Margaret hasn't changed," Archie says to me as he looks around, observing the same chaos I'm seeing.

Kids running everywhere. Singles mingling by the fireplace. Dr. Sharpe included. He's fresh blood in a small town, and age is no discriminator of interest. Several of Margaret's generation are in the house, but Margaret herself is visiting with Tripp. Or at least, she was...

"Oh no, here she comes." Archie tries to turn his back to Margaret, but I've learned it's best to know what's coming your way.

Margaret is blazing a trail through the people as she beelines for us. Besides a quick greeting when we first arrived, we haven't spoken with her.

"There you are. Have you knocked him on the head yet?" she asks as she peers at us over her glasses.

"No, Margaret, not yet."

She huffs. "The evening is young. It could still happen."

"I'd rather it didn't," Archie pipes up. "Hey, you never told us the details of the crash. Did you get to actually see the plane wreck?"

Margaret perks up at the question. "Did I see the plane wreck?! It spilled my lunchtime tea! Stained my cream doily."

Archie leans over to whisper in my ear, "I don't think I want to know what a doily is." His warm breath distracts me from his ridiculous comment.

We're soon regaled with a detailed explanation of Margaret walking out her back door to find a plane in her backyard.

Eventually, she's called away by someone asking where to put a Jell-O salad. "Ten more minutes, then the games start," she warns us as she walks away.

"Do you suppose we should get that hauled away?" Archie asks, turning to look at the wreckage in question.

"Don't look at me. I sold my plane trailer last week," I whisper back.

"Smart-ass. I'm going to go look at it just real quick before the game starts."

My heart lurches at the thought of him being in that plane. But I rein it in. "Sounds great. That will give me more time to limber up."

"You're not winning this one." He gives a jaunty salute, then hurries toward the plane.

I watch him pick his way through the glass until he's standing at the front, where the nose is resting on the ground. I don't know much—or anything—about planes, but the landing gear looks as though it's bent backward. Like that plane crashed without even trying to catch itself with its hands.

A gentleman with white hair, a limp in his step, and a Leatherman hanging off his belt follows after Archie.

I don't recognize the man. I wonder if it's Margaret's latest acquisition. The woman gets around. I want to know how many people she has dated in her lifetime, because I do not know how she does it. It's exhausting to watch, much less participate in.

Twenty minutes later, Margaret has the megaphone out, calling everyone over to the starting line.

Bocce is a loose term. War would be more accurate. It resembles more of a hockey game than anything else.

"Maybe you should sit this one out," I say to Archie. "I don't want you getting hurt. You're still recovering."

His hand presses against my lower back. "If you think I'm going to miss this... I'm scared to find out if I've changed that much."

Eight players line up. And then as it quiets down, we spy the ball that we have to get closest to. It's sitting precariously balanced on the dangling tail of the plane wreckage.

"This is going to end badly," someone else says.

I can't help but agree with them.

Thirty minutes later, we're on the second game. The second game is always more intense. Dan won the first game, so he's guaranteed to lose the second. Everyone is out to sabotage him, except for Archie, who seems to be taking special joy in foiling my own game. With bocce extreme, physical interference is allowed as long as it doesn't result in personal injury. The rule used to be simply "Physical interference is allowed," but then Margaret whacked the mayor with her cane. An addendum was added.

Archie takes it to the limit, stepping in the way and

ruining my toss, yelling right before I release the ball, whispering things in my ear. All in all, I've been playing lousy with him distracting me.

It's the only reason I start fighting dirty. "Wow, is it hot this evening or what?" I lift my shirt to fan some air, making sure I catch Archie's eye as he prepares for his shot.

He misses, and his ball falls short of the target ball.

"Meyer," he growls at me.

I look at him with my best innocent face and step forward for my own throw.

I launch the ball, but when Archie steps a foot out in front of me and I trip, the ball goes flying upward, sailing over the fence into the neighbor's yard. I hear a thump on the other side and only hope that it didn't land on someone's head.

I stand up straight and turn to look at him. "You made me lose the ball."

He smiles slowly. "Oh, did I do that? I hadn't realized you were walking this way to throw it."

"I wasn't walking anywhere to throw it. You purposely tripped me."

Suddenly, Margaret is here, her head on a swivel as she watches us argue back and forth. "Now, children, there's no reason to fight about this. You'll have to go make sure the neighbors are okay."

Apparently, she had the same thought I did: another drive to the ER.

"You'll just have to go to retrieve it."

I plant my hands on my hips and stare at Archie. He

141

smiles back and holds out his hand in a grand gesture. He's enjoying himself far too much.

And I'm afraid that I am, too.

Chapter Thirteen

"I'm going to go for a hike this morning. I need to clear my head," Archie announces.

After a late night at Margaret's—she'd brought out the karaoke machine after bocce ball—we'd come home and slept in late this morning. One of the perks of running my own business. No time clock to punch. I can make up the time by staying up later tonight. Probably not a great habit to build, but I'll worry about that later.

Archie is wearing jeans and a thick plaid sweatshirt with a gray hood attached. He looks positively rural. I can't believe he actually owns one now. It must have been in his travel bag I retrieved from the airplane. He used to say he would never be caught dead in plaid, yet here he stands.

"Okay, do you need to borrow my pepper spray?"

His lips quirk to the side. "I think I'll pass. Thanks for thinking of me, but I've spent as much time with your pepper spray as I ever want to."

"I don't want anyone taking advantage of you," I tease.

But his smile disappears, and now, he's frowning at me.

"It's not something to joke about, Meyer. I'm still mad that something happened to you and that it's something you think about still. That was my fault."

I roll my eyes because, otherwise, I'll start crying. "I wish Kingston hadn't said that to you. It's just not true."

"I wish I could remember these things." He grunts in frustration and yanks his hood up over his head, as if he's expecting a heavy rain on his hike.

With it being late spring in Oregon, it is a very real possibility. You have to be ready for all four seasons if you do any outdoor activities here.

"Get out of here and stop worrying about things that you can't remember. It will come back, I promise." Hopefully, I can deliver on that promise.

Archie walks into the kitchen and leans over to kiss me on the cheek.

"As soon as I remember, I'm going to fix whatever this is between us."

"That's very sweet of you."

When he fixes it, it will be me staring at taillights as he drives out of here. And it scares me how much that hurts to think about.

He heads out on his walk, and I pour the last of the coffee into my travel mug, even though I will be staying home today. I learned long ago that having an open mug on a craft desk ends with coffee everywhere and ruined hours of work.

The front door opens, and I wonder if Archie has forgotten something important, like his pants, but it's more likely that he's forgotten his music.

"Is Archie home?" The voice startles me.

I jump and turn around to find my sister standing there. She looks strange—like she's missing something. That's when I realize there isn't a child attached to her.

"What are you doing? Where are all your children?"

"Is he home?" she prods, ignoring my questions.

"No, he went on a hike just a minute ago. I'm surprised you didn't pass him on your way in."

I grab a second cup and split half of my coffee with hers. She takes it when I hand it to her.

"Thank you." Her usual energetic voice sounds subdued.

"Is everything okay?"

Oh no. She's dying. She's here to tell me it's terminal.

She takes the cup of coffee, walks into the living room, and sits down. Something must be horribly wrong. But before I can think of worst-case scenario options A through Z, she explains why she's here.

"I'm here for an intervention with you, Meyer."

"An intervention?"

"Yes. Watching you last night was painful."

"My throwing arm does leave something to be desired," I agree.

She sighs, and it's a nice, well-practiced, obviously often-used sigh. "I'm talking about the way you were looking at Archie."

My legs tighten, and I raise my coffee cup up to my

lips. I don't take a sip. I just use it as an excuse to not speak yet.

She continues, "I am worried about you. It looks like you're falling for him all over again."

I sigh now, though it's not near the level of hers. I think I could practice my whole life and never be as good at it as she is.

"There's nothing going on. He still doesn't remember."

"That's what I mean. I'm scared that you're going to fall for him, and then he will remember everything. Then, you'll have your heart broken a second time. I'm scared you're going to get hurt, Meyer, and I'm just here to see what I can do to help. Do you want him to come stay at our house until Holly comes and gets him? Do you know when she will be here?"

I shake my head. "It's fine. This is what's best for now. And I really do appreciate your concern."

She stares at me with the signature Bailey look.

"Okay, fine. If I'm completely honest with myself, it's something I'm scared of, too."

Bailey reaches across the arm of the chair and squeezes my hand. She's the one who sat through the divorce. She listened to many a cryfest.

"I'm afraid that I'm going to have a hard time sending him away again. It's like we've been given this restart. And I know it's completely selfish of me to want to pretend like everything is okay, but maybe this is our chance! Maybe this is a fresh start. This time, I can do everything right!"

Bailey shakes her head. "One person doing everything right doesn't save a marriage between two people. It just delays the inevitable. Look, I'm sure you've matured and grown up since you and Archie split. So, maybe Archie has, too. But don't you think he deserves to start at the same level as you? If you are wanting another chance, he needs to know the truth. All of it."

I lean back and fold my arms across my chest. Petulance is practically stamped across my forehead. "The doctor said we shouldn't force him to remember."

"Then, you need to let him go home to his mother and heal. Then, you can revisit this after he regains his memories. Because what you're doing right now? It's not fair to him. And it's going to crush your heart in the end."

"Don't you have some children to parent?"

Bailey tucks her legs underneath her. "Nope. Dan has the day off and is giving me a kid break. So, I decided to come parent you instead."

"I hate when you do that."

"Or do you only hate it when I'm right?"

"That too," I admit.

We sit and stare at each other. We engage in a *don't blink* contest. I win, as usual, but it feels like I've lost.

"Fine. I'll call Holly again."

"Good. You know I like Archie. Heck, I named a kid after him. But it doesn't mean I want to watch you get your heart broken twice from him. I wish things had worked out for you guys, but I really, really want you to be happy. And if he wasn't willing to stay the first time, I don't want him to leave you a second time."

I open my mouth to refute that he left me, but the words stick in my throat. My family doesn't know how two-sided our fight was. Even Bailey, who listened to me vomit my soul after our divorce, doesn't know the words I screamed to seal the deal.

"Why don't you just go?"

Because it scares me that maybe I hold just as much responsibility in our separation as he does. That maybe I can't place my enormous anger solely at his door.

Nope. Not ready to say that. Not now. Maybe not ever. Because it took me almost a year to admit it to myself.

❀

After Bailey leaves, I disappear into my office and begin to work.

I've only gotten about fifteen minutes of work done before Archie pokes his head in, informing me that he's going on a drive with Tripp and is going to show him around the area and possibly go on a short hike.

Once he's gone, I turn on an audiobook and listen as a plucky regency heroine falls in love. Of course, she knows all the right things to say, and it's the exact fantasy my mind needs as I make earrings.

Three hours later, I glance at the clock and realize that I haven't had lunch yet and that Archie could be home at any moment. Before I fill the hunger need, I need to take care of something and channel my inner *regency-era-heroine* spunk.

I call my mother-in-law.

"Holly? You need to come get Archie." I hang up.

She has to be screening my calls. I've tried calling and

texting multiple times and still no answer. What could possibly be more important than her baby?

I need Holly to be here.

I turn up the volume on my earbuds and begin labeling packages. I do not need to be thinking about Archie, his teasing and his hands, his competitiveness, and the way he ribs me in a fun way, not a hurtful way. The guy is firmly under my skin, and I've literally opened the door and invited him in.

It's time for him to go home—before I do something I'll regret.

Chapter Fourteen

My fingers are sore, my regency romance hero and heroine are living happily ever after, and my packages are sitting in a basket by the door, waiting to be delivered to Janice in the morning.

Archie still isn't home, and I'm hoping that Tripp doesn't turn out to be a serial killer.

I head into the laundry room and pull out my sparkling cider from my secret stash—as if I am able to hide it from myself—and pour some into a glass full of ice cubes.

The front door cracks open, and I frantically look around for somewhere to hide my glass.

"Oh, is that for me?" Archie asks as he walks into the kitchen.

Busted.

Archie loves sparkling cider as much as I do, which is why I thought about hiding it.

"How was your hike? You may have one teeny-tiny sip," I tell him as he pulls the glass from my hand and proceeds to drink the entire contents.

He coughs. "Wow, I was thirsty after that hike."

He passes back the glass, and the twinkle in his eye is unmistakable. I carefully pick up an ice cube from the glass, making sure Archie is watching my every move. Then, I step forward and reach for the collar of his shirt. He jumps back out of my reach.

"But, honey, I thought you were hot from that hike! I'm just trying to cool you down."

I half-heartedly swipe at him before I pop the ice cube into my mouth.

We're both grinning like fools.

He closes the distance in two steps. Then, his hands are on me, and he's kissing me.

Happy, shocked, and scared, I kiss him back. It's habit. That's what I tell myself. Pure instinct right here.

Archie helps that ice cube melt even faster.

It's so right, him holding me, kissing me. How did I get here? I don't want to even think about it. All I care about right now is how right this is. How much I've *missed* him. How much I wish I had fought for us.

I moan as he twirls a lock of hair around his fingers, taking his time to kiss me. I don't have to wonder if it would be like this with anyone else. Archie is the only one I've ever felt like this with, and I find myself being a staunch believer in the term *soul mates* at this moment.

Lip mates.

His fingers find their way to the button earring on my right ear, and he traces the edge of it, sending sparks shooting down my neck.

A loud crash of thunder snaps me out of the trance I'm in. I jump back, and Archie lets me go.

"We can't—we—"

A frantic meow and a screech interrupt what I was going to say.

Thunder rumbles again. A spring storm.

"Gatsby," we both say at the same time.

Gatsby hates storms.

Splitting up, we spend a few frantic minutes looking for Gatsby. Unfortunately, he's not in his usual haunts.

"I can't find Gatsby!" I say when I bump into Archie in the hall.

"Do you think he went into the garage?"

"I'm not sure. I'll check."

"I'll go check in the backyard."

We go our separate ways, and I quickly discover that Gatsby is not in the garage—or he's an excellent hider.

"Meyer, he's out here!" Archie's shout reaches my ears where I am in the living room. It's muted, and I have a sinking feeling.

Hurrying outside, I stand under the cover of the patio overhang. Archie's standing next to the birdbath and pointing at Gatsby up the tree. He's a wet furball, clinging to the branch above Archie's head.

"The greedy guy was probably trying to steal a bird out of that birdbath when the storm hit," Archie says.

"He takes after his father!" I call out.

I really don't want to go out there in the torrential

downpour. Maybe Archie could just grab him and bring him in, and we can get him dried off in front of the heater.

"Here, Gatsby!" Archie calls to him, reaching up for him.

Gatsby doesn't budge.

"How about a nice treat inside?"

Gatsby knows the word *treat*. You can whisper the word five miles away, and he would come running. But it's still not enough to break through his storm-induced terror.

"Gatsby, it's wet and cold. I want to go inside and kiss my wife. Come down."

My heart jumps around at his words and his tone.

The cat doesn't budge.

"That's it," Archie snaps. "If you won't come down, then I'm just going to have to grab you."

He glances around, looking for something to stand on to reach the lowest branch that Gatsby is sitting on. We limbed the tree when we first moved in, and the three years we've been here have added some height.

Archie sets a foot on top of the birdbath directly below the branch.

"Archie! You'll fall! Let me get a stepladder."

"It'll be fine! I don't want to stay out here any longer than necessary." He's standing on the stone bowl now and calmly reaching toward the cat.

"Archie! It's not attached. It just sits on top."

At first, I'm worried he can't hear me, but then he answers as he latches onto the cat. "Don't worry. I have excellent balance."

The last word is cut off as the stone bowl shoots out from under him. He falls backward off the bath and lands flat on his back, still holding onto Gatsby.

I run out to him, ignoring the torrential rain and the fact that I'm barefoot.

"Archie!" I crouch down next to him.

He's not moving. His eyes are closed tight, and he has a death grip on the cat.

"Wake up, Archie!" There's a slight flinch, but his eyes remain closed. "Archie!"

His lips part, and words tumble out even though his eyes are closed. "Stop screaming in my ear."

"I'm not screaming. Who's screaming?" I laugh calmly, collectedly—okay, maybe it's hysterical.

"You're screaming," he groans and finally opens his eyes.

Okay, maybe I am screaming a little.

"I thought you were unconscious."

"Don't worry. I felt all of it." He sits up and swipes the rain from his face with an equally wet arm. He looks around the yard, as though looking for the culprit of his fall.

I glance at the imprint on the ground. "You hit your head on a root. This is bad."

Archie stands up and looks at me. It's hard to see his face in the darkness. I can't tell if there's blood anywhere. But I'm glad to see that he's standing.

"Come in on the porch so I can see what happened. We'll head to the hospital."

"I don't need a hospital." He says the last word deliberately, as if he's trying to convince himself that he doesn't need a hospital.

"Do you think there's blood?" I ask.

He shakes his head haltingly and follows me to the house. Gatsby is tucked under his arm.

"I don't want you to have a bad concussion. You've hit your head one too many times lately. Are you sure we shouldn't go to the hospital?"

I clasp his elbow, and Gatsby takes a swipe at me. The little traitor. I lead the way into the house and study Archie's head under the laundry-room light.

I carefully look at the back of his head, inspecting anywhere that there might be a cut. It feels like there might be a small lump on the back of his head, and I press gently on it.

"Does this hurt?" I ask.

"Not too bad. It's tender, that's for sure."

"Okay. Do you think we should go get it checked out?"

Archie is still staring at me with a wide look, and I'm just about to say that we are going to the hospital when he answers me. "I think I just need to rest my head. I'm dizzy a little bit. But my vision is fine."

"What can I do to help you?"

He rubs the back of his head and answers in a snarky tone, "Why don't you just make sure that Gatsby stays inside? I'm going to wash this dirt off, then go to bed."

As if it's my fault. I said he should use a stepladder. I warned him he would fall.

I plant my hands on my hips.

He walks past me quietly. I trail behind him and stop abruptly when he stands behind the blue couch for a moment. He studies it, then snorts and turns down the hall.

I watch as he disappears into the bathroom. Hopefully, the warm shower helps.

Gatsby is nowhere to be seen, and I'm left staring at the hallway my husband disappeared down.

I made out with my ex-husband tonight. And now, I'm not sure what to do about it.

Go to bed, I suppose. Sleep always gives me answers. And so I climb into bed, listening to the sound of the shower running. I try not to think about who's in that shower and how good it felt to kiss him again. How his hands felt like home.

A sexy, hot home.

I rub my hands over my face, trying to get the image out of my mind before I go to sleep. Because if I'm not careful, that's what I'll dream of. And dreams are a dangerous place, where truths are revealed.

The bathroom door opens, and Archie marches out. He's actually dressed. Miracles still happen, folks. "Where's my phone? Have you seen it?"

It's the first time he's been concerned about it since he's been here.

"No, I'm not sure. Do you need it right now?"

He pivots to stare at me. "Yes."

"Okay, then." I shake my head and turn to look at the mantel. The phone is sitting right next to the small TV.

"Oh, it blended in with that. They're both the same size," Archie says sarcastically.

"Are you sure you're okay?" I ask.

"I'm fine. I just need some sleep."

I nod, even though I don't agree. I'd rather he sit his butt down in the car so I can drive him to the hospital and make sure everything is fine.

"Do you want me to call Dr. Sharpe?" It's not like he has a life in town. He'd seemed slightly desperate for companionship if he didn't mind pepper-spraying hikers.

"No," Archie practically barks. "I'll call him. Thanks."

With that, he disappears into the guest bedroom, and I'm left to worry about his second head injury.

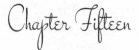

Chapter Fifteen

The next morning, I get up early because my fitful sleep was plagued with very real dreams of Archie. Or maybe they were memories. It doesn't matter. I'm not going to dwell on it. The point is, I need a shower.

I grab my clothes and stumble toward the bathroom. I hear Archie's voice muffled through his bedroom door just as I reach for the bathroom door. I had creepily peeked through the guest bedroom door multiple times last night to make sure I could hear his deep breathing. It wasn't quite a snore, but it wasn't a whisper-soft breath either.

In between reassuring myself that he was still alive, I'd fall into a fitful sleep plagued with dreams of Archie.

He must have heard me walk into the hall. I turn to the guest room. I wonder if I should have forced him to go to the hospital last night. Heavy breathing isn't necessarily a sign of good health. As I reach for the doorknob, his voice rings out clearly.

"Yes, Mom, I know." His voice is urgent.

Either he's dreaming or talking on the phone. Not sure what to do, I freeze until his voice rings out again.

"I don't know what I'm going to do!"

He must be having a nightmare. It doesn't sound like a dream to me!

I grasp the knob, ready to open the door and go wake him up. He doesn't need to be thrashing around. His stitches are starting to dissolve. I don't want anything to tear prematurely.

Another trip to the hospital will probably not endear us to Dr. Sharpe.

"I remember everything!"

Three little words. Three little words that could mean so many different things, but they have me pausing in my quest to save him from a nightmare.

He remembers everything?

I stand perfectly still, curious to see if he will continue on.

"I know, Mom. Last night, after I hit my head, it was like it came in a rush. I don't really remember the plane crash, but I'm no longer missing those two years. I even remember why I was flying out here."

I stand frozen, wondering if I should barge in, point at him, and yell, *Faker!* But that feels a little bit too abrupt, especially since he's probably still processing.

I don't know if I feel relief or if I'm even more anxious now that he remembers.

What am I going to do with the man in my house who remembers that we're divorced? How do I explain that I was playing along to heal him? How do I get him to not accuse me of trying to trick him into marriage again? I'll run away. That's the best option for this situation.

There's no salvaging it. I'll pack my backpack that I've had since freshman year of college and be on the first bus out of Green Lake.

Ha, that's funny. I would prefer hitchhiking over public transportation. Buses make me carsick.

Or I could take my car that I own. But it doesn't seem quite as dramatic to run away in your own car.

"She's been taking care of me, Mom."

Between the pauses and his tone, I finally realize that he's not having a dream. He's talking on the phone to his mother. The very same mother who has been screening my calls and texts and my requests for her to come pick up her son. At least now I know her phone is still working and she's not dead in a ditch somewhere. She just doesn't feel like helping me up here.

"I know I should tell her."

Yes, he should.

"But I feel like this is me getting a second chance."

Wait, what?

He continues speaking as if I'm not having an existential crisis in the hall. "What if I pretend a little longer and see how she feels toward me?"

I hold my breath as I wait for him to speak again.

"Yes, I know it could backfire. But I came out here to try and see if her feelings had changed. If I tell her now that I remember, she'll send me straight back to Arizona, and I'll never get that chance!"

I slowly release the breath I was holding. There's so much to unpack in just a few short sentences. But I know that I need to get out of the hall before he catches me eavesdropping.

"I just need a little time to show her how much she means to me, show her that we could be good together again. Show her that I've matured. If you could just stall a little longer, I'll find a way to break it to her easy, in a way that she won't be mad at me—all over again, that is."

I carefully tiptoe backward toward the shower. I avoid stepping on the third plank, which always creaks.

I slip into the bathroom and start the shower. I always do my best thinking there. And I have a *lot* of thinking to do.

The warm water is almost uncomfortable; it's so hot. But I'm too lost in thought to adjust the temperature.

My top questions I've come up with in the shower are, *Do I want a second chance with Archie? Does he deserve a second chance with me? Do I deserve him?*

Because if he flew all the way back here simply for me, that means his feelings toward me aren't contrived. They aren't a thing of the past like I had assumed. I'm not the only one harboring feelings for their ex.

Which leads to the question of, *Do I let him get away with playing pretend?* Or do I call him out on it the second he steps foot into the kitchen this morning?

I could reveal it in a big *aha* moment, casually slip it into conversation. *Would you like cream with your coffee? Would you like a ticket back to Arizona? Jelly or honey on your toast?*

And then, between the shampoo and the conditioner, I have another brainstorm.

What if I go along with his pretend? There are so many interesting things that I could do. If he is going to pretend like he still has amnesia, I can help him remember by reminding him of all his favorite things. Cue my best evil laugh.

I can remind him that he loves grocery shopping—Archie hates grocery shopping.

That he goes for a run every morning—Archie abhors running.

That he only wears monochromatic clothes—he would only ever be caught dead in a gray sweatsuit.

I rinse my hair and hurry out of the shower. My brilliantly evil scheme takes shape in my mind as I get dressed.

Stopping myself from smiling is surprisingly difficult. Perhaps I missed my life's calling of being a villainess. Thankfully, it's never too late to change.

But as I step into the hallway, I sigh heavily, knowing that petty revenge is *not* the answer.

Trudging to the kitchen, I stare forlornly at the empty coffeepot. Next, I open the fridge and stare at the contents. Maybe those leftover ketchup packets have the answer.

Or maybe I need to caffeinate.

"Good morning." Archie's voice is tentative at best. Funny, since he sounded so confident on the phone with his mother.

I flip open the lid to the coffeepot and pour water inside, then turn around to face him.

"Good morning, hubby."

His flinch is barely discernible, but it's there.

"I'm just making a pot of coffee. Would you like some?"

"Sure." He walks into the kitchen, grabs a glass out of the cupboard, and fills it with tap water.

I can feel his eyes on me as I dump the coffee grounds in. The quiet sound of his sipping is the only thing that breaks the silence. I punch the start button on the coffeepot and turn to face him.

He sets the glass down with a click and folds his arms across his chest.

"How's your head feeling this morning?"

He reaches back and rubs the back of his head, causing his arm muscles to bunch as he does so. "Not too bad. There were rocks under my head where I fell."

"Well, I've always wondered if your head or rock is harder, and now I know. But I just wonder if we should go into the hospital so you can get checked out, to make sure that no more mental damage was done. Maybe they could do a CT scan." I suggest with a smile. It's probably an evil smile if I could see myself. But I'm not stupid enough to put a mirror in my kitchen. I do not need to see what I look like when I'm frazzled while cooking.

"I don't think that's necessary," Archie replies. "I really don't think more doctor visits are going to help me at this point."

I stare at him. If I stare long enough, maybe he'll spit out the truth. He shifts his weight back and forth, and I have to wonder if it's killing him to lie.

But then, his face breaks into a grin, and he suggests, "Why don't we go on a hike today?"

I scowl. "I have a meeting at nine this morning."

Archie shrugs and turns to grab two cups from the cupboard. He pours cream into both of them. "I just thought maybe some fresh air would help me start remembering things."

"It didn't seem to help you remember things last night."

"Yeah, that's because I was drowning in the rain."

"You've had fresh air multiple times this week. What about your new best friend, Tripp?"

A smirk steals his face.

He grabs the coffeepot and fills both of our cups, then passes one to me.

"Just one teeny-tiny little hike?"

"I can tell you're going to pester me about this, so I'll do the only thing I can at the moment. One small, tiny hike. We'll walk down and get the mail together."

Archie laughs.

He takes a slow sip of his coffee, keeping his eyes on me. "I think I'm going to need a longer walk than the ten feet to the mailbox."

"Hey now, our driveway is not short." I walk around him to peer out the kitchen window that faces the driveway. "That's at least fifty feet."

Archie comes to stand behind me, and I can feel the heat radiating off his chest against my back as he looks out the window with me.

"Thirty at best."

He doesn't move back, but he's still not touching me.

And Archie remembers. Which means he has to remember the epic fight we had, even though he's willingly close to me. I step back and *accidentally* elbow him straight in the ribs.

"Oops. I didn't know you were standing so close."

I step to the side but make sure that I step on top of his foot on the way. He manages to keep all of his coffee in the cup, but I can't say the same about myself. I now have a stain on my running shorts.

"You'll have to help yourself to some breakfast here while I go to my meeting. I'm meeting Willa at The Egg Crack at nine. Our meetings usually last an hour or two."

Archie glances at the clock, glances at me. "That's still an hour and a half away," he says, being annoyingly practical.

"I'm stopping at the post office, and I have to try to take some pictures on my way. I've been told that my social media presence is completely lacking. Willa is thorough."

Archie looks at me. "Has it been good to have her as a PR manager?"

His genuine concern in the question has me actually pausing to think about it.

Not counting the big deal that Willa landed for me that's pressing down on my soul, she has done wonders for my business. It had taken nearly all the marketing work off of my shoulders when I hired her. I've experienced incredible growth, she manages all my influencers, all my advertising, any campaign in sales, any local businesses that I sell through. She handles the people side of the business, and I get to just enjoy creating.

I tell all of this to Archie. And he listens as he takes sips of coffee.

"It sounds like a really good fit for you," he says with a smile.

"I think so," I agree. "She handles everything for me, and I don't know if it's a good thing or not, but I feel as if we are friends sometimes. I like to think that she enjoys working with me."

Archie snorts. "Everyone loves working with you. They'd be out of their minds not to."

"You don't like working with me." I say this with raised eyebrows.

He looks slightly chagrined. It is true, though. He can't stand working with me because I have a hard time sticking with my original decisions. I want to make sure that everyone is happy with the outcome.

"As much as I would love to argue about who does and does not like to work with me, I need to get going. I have to run errands after my meeting, too." I point a finger at him. "No more falling. Tell Gatsby he can take care of himself if he goes and gets stuck in the tree. It would serve him right."

We both know I don't mean that. I'm always a sucker for that stinking cat. And I will be forever pulling him out of a tight space until it eventually kills me.

Because I know for sure that Gatsby will outlive me.

It isn't until I sit down to brunch with Willa that I realize I stood there in the kitchen, talking with a very cognizant Archie and explaining my business to him, and didn't feel a single bit of pressure, only pure interest.

Willa is talking a mile a minute, and I don't have time

to contemplate why Archie's shift in attitude should mean so much to me.

By the end of the day, I know exactly what I want to do. Somewhere amid my supply shopping, I determined I needed to stand my ground. I'm pretty sure I was in the sewing section at the time.

And by standing my ground, I mean not letting Archie get away with keeping it a secret that he remembers.

I'm just not sure if I have the guts to go through with it. There are so many things that I *could* do, so much fun that I *could* have. But I just don't know if I possess that level of sadism.

I open the door and step inside. I see Archie standing in the kitchen, listening to some pop music while he cooks dinner. Whatever he's making smells amazing. He's always been the better cook out of the two of us, that's for sure. I stand for a minute and savor the smell as I decide that, no, I can't trick him back. It seems unfair. Instead, I should just confront him with the truth. But I can almost taste that basil and Parmesan. I slam the door. I'm so tired of having to slam that thing. I'll get it fixed first thing when Archie's gone.

It sounds like I'm angry every time I come home. When the reality is, usually I just want to nap.

Archie turns around and grins at me. "I made some dinner!"

"It smells delicious." Now, I need to shock him with the truth. *Tell him that I know.*

"Can you grab the wine glasses down from the top shelf?" Archie asks me.

I'm about to protest as I see him lifting a tall glass bottle. He's already forgotten that I've given up drinking. So much for believing a second chance could turn out differently and that he would actually pay attention to what I want.

But then I see the label on the bottom and realize he's pouring sparkling cider. And now, I don't even want to confront him with the truth, not if he's going to keep being sweet like this. Maybe we can both play pretend.

Because that's healthy thinking, Meyer.

He passes a full glass to me, and then he turns the music down. I take a small sip as he comes back to stand right in front of me. He has a serious look on his face as his eyes ping-pong back and forth over mine. They are always searching for something.

"Thank you for thinking of this." I lift the glass a little and take another sip.

He must've found my stash, the one I keep in the laundry room cupboard. Because sometimes, a girl just needs a little treat.

"You know, I'm feeling a lot better. I was a little worried that you would come in tonight and get mad at me for cooking."

"It did cross my mind, but then I smelled the food," I reply with a smile.

"The point is, I really think it would be good for me if we started getting on with life as usual."

He tilts his head toward me. He's waiting for me to say yes. I narrow my eyes at him and think about what 'life as usual' would mean.

He remembers that we are divorced.

And I'm about to open my mouth and shout my own *aha* moment, which I've always wanted to do, but then I think about that fun little list I made in my mind while eating brunch with Willa.

I frown at Archie. "But life isn't normal right now, is it?" I enunciate every word, as if I am auditioning for a Broadway play. *She's got emotion, folks.*

"You mean, because of my accident?" His fake innocent face isn't fooling me.

"Well, it's not as if you remember everything, is it? Life can't go back to usual just yet." I sip my sparkling cider and sniff the basil wafting through the air.

"But if I go back to our regular routine, it might help jog my memory. We cook dinner more often. Maybe I can find some work to do here that would keep me busy. Something to feel normal."

What he's saying is, he wants to continue to play house together. That he's not going to tell me the truth—at least not now.

Maybe he just needs a little bit of time to get up the courage. Even I can understand that. It would be awkward to wake up one day and realize that you're living in your ex-spouse's house and that you've been acting like everything is completely normal.

It isn't exactly easy circumstances to navigate. I can appreciate that. But if he isn't going to tell me the truth, that gives me some free license to make our 'normal' a little bit different than he 'remembers' it.

I look him in the eye and smile. "You're right. Maybe a little bit more routine to get back to normal will help you remember."

Something in my tone has him looking skeptical, so he's not sure what's going to come of it. Good. It's his turn to be jumpy.

And my turn for a little payback.

Chapter Sixteen

My brilliant plan of payback is not off to a good start.

I open my eyes the next morning to discover there's someone else in my bed other than Gatsby. "Archie, we might be going back to normal, but we're still not going to bump that head of yours. Get off my pillow."

He grins and rolls back a few inches. "When did you start sleeping in the middle of the bed?"

He's still so close. I can see the beginning of stubble on his chin. He has to shave every other day, otherwise things get hairy.

I prop up on an elbow and stare at him. "I've always slept in the middle of the bed. That must just be a strange memory you can't recall."

His lips twitch. "Well, don't get too used to it, because pretty soon, this head of mine is gonna be healed. I just wanted to snuggle you for a little bit this morning."

I press my lips together to keep from snapping out a retort. This is getting out of hand. I jump out of bed and grab my walking clothes. I'm going to need some fresh air to hash out my brilliant, sinister, dastardly evil plan.

The walk around the lake does little to clear my head. Instead, I stub my toe on a rock. Then, on my way back, I accidentally step in a giant puddle and splash mud all over myself. By the time I trudge into the house, I'm grumpy, muddy, and still obsessing over what I did to deserve a stubbed toe and an ex-husband in my house— and in my bed.

Jumping in the shower after my walk helps me avoid Archie a little longer.

I made sure he was still in the kitchen, making breakfast, when I snuck in here. If he wants to go back to *normal*—him making breakfast every day—I will happily take it. He's a great cook.

I open the shower curtain to step out and grab my towel, but it's not there.

I check the clothes hamper. Empty.

"Archie!" I call, not too loud because I'm not sure I actually want him to answer.

The bathroom door slams open, bouncing off the wall, like Archie has been waiting for this moment his whole life. I jerk the shower curtain back to shield me. Only my eyes are visible. Archie has a bright smile on his face.

"I don't remember moving my towel," I mumble against the now-cold shower curtain.

"Oh, I just thought I'd help by doing some laundry this morning while you were out on your walk. I must have forgotten to bring the towels back in." He grins.

He did *not* forget.

"Could you bring me one, please?" My *please* is said in a tone that leaves no room for argument.

"Be right back!"

His peppy step makes me want to yell at him. Or maybe laugh.

He's back fast enough that I wonder if he had the towels sitting right outside the door and I didn't notice.

"Here you go!" He stands in the bathroom and holds the towel out, as though I'm going to step out of the shower and let him dry me off.

"Hand it here."

"Why don't you come here and let me help you?" His eyebrows waggle up and down.

"Why don't you pass that towel here if you know what's good for you?"

"Is that a promise?"

Keeping the shower curtain tucked around me, I step out and snatch the towel from him, then hurry back to the safety of the shower.

His laughter echoes in the bathroom as he leaves.

That evil, little...

I hurry and dry off, then get dressed in my shorts and pink off-the-shoulder blouse. I march out of the bathroom, wet towel in hand and retribution in my mind.

I find him in the kitchen, making a pot of coffee—probably his second one of the day.

I grab the ends of the towel, twisting until it's tight, and then I let it fly. I snap him on the left butt cheek with a crack.

He yelps and spins around, barely dodging my second snap.

"Meyer!" he roars.

But I'm already laughing too hard to get away as he runs for me, scooping me up in his arms and prying the towel from my hands. "You are the worst towel snapper."

"Or am I the best?" I cackle as we stumble to the rug in the living room and end up in a tangle of limbs as he tries to snap me with the towel.

I'm laughing too hard to try and steal the towel back, and despite him having the towel, I know Archie can't snap a towel to save his life.

"I'm going to have a bruise!" he complains.

"You were being cheeky about the towels!" I snap back with a laugh.

He releases me and reaches back to rub the spot I snapped. "Well, now, you're the one who got cheeky with the towels."

I roll over and flop backward onto the rug, gasping for air through the laughter.

Archie sits up and pulls the end of the towel out from under me. "That's it. No more towel for you. I can't trust you with this thing." He stomps off to the bathroom and hangs it up.

I'm still laughing uncontrollably by the time he gets back.

He stands there, trying to frown at me with his hands on his hips. "I'm hurt, and you're laughing."

"Oh, come on, as if anything could hurt those buns of steel."

"I might have a bruise. Maybe you should kiss it."

"I am not kissing your ass."

"I'm not sharing my coffee."

I jump up and hurry toward him. "You mean, my coffee?"

"Why is it your coffee?" he asks as we push and pull at each other as we try to make it back to the kitchen.

I frantically search my brain for a reason as to why it's my coffee. "Because I bought it at the grocery store!"

"We buy everything at the grocery store."

"I mean, I was the one who went into the grocery store and paid for it," I explain as I hip-check him just as he's reaching for a coffee cup.

"But you always do the grocery shopping."

Inspiration hits at the same time Archie does. A tickle of my ribs has me flinching as he beats me to the cupboard.

"*You* do all the grocery shopping now," I say slyly. "You must not remember that part."

I can feel my smile turning practically splitting my cheeks as Archie slowly turns around.

"What?"

"Oh, yes. You love grocery shopping now. In fact, it would probably be good for you to start doing the things you love to do. It might help you regain your memory. I have a list on the fridge. You can grab those things today since you want everything to go back to normal." I smile sweetly as I reach past a stunned Archie and grab my favorite mug.

Some people hate slow traffic. Some people hate snakes. Archie hates grocery shopping. And it is my sincerest joy to trap him into it.

I'm waiting, standing in line at the post office, behind someone who has never heard of a tracking number before. She's explaining her fourteen previous addresses to Janice, the mail lady, and I know I'll be stuck here, waiting a while.

I'm still elated about this morning. My chest feels like it's on fire—but it's a happy burn. My cheeks hurt from smiling as I remember our morning together. Knowing that he's fully himself. That he's there because he *wants* to be. My hope meter is off the charts.

I pull out my phone and send off a text to Archie.

Me: I remembered we need oat milk. Please pick it up when you go to the grocery store. Thanks, sweetie!

I barely resist adding a little devil emoji. Although, it is tempting.

"And then we moved to Fayetteville—" the woman explains.

I'm not convinced that Janice is even awake for this explanation.

Archie: Oat milk? Who milks the oats?

Me: And chocolate ice cream. I need some of that, too.

Archie: You want oat milk, but full-dairy ice cream? Or do you want me to go milk an avocado and make ice cream out of that?

Me: While the idea of watching you milk an avocado is intriguing...I think I'll pass.

Me: They DO make avocado ice cream. But you'd better get Tillamook. It's the best.

Archie: At least you still have good ice cream taste…

The customer in front of me finally leaves, and I heft my basket onto the counter.

"Good afternoon. How can I help you?" Janice asks.

"I'm great. I just need to ship these packages."

Three, two, one.

"That's a mountain of them."

"Yes, it sure is."

After painstakingly weighing each package, she labels them. It's not a quick process by any means.

"Do you need any stamps today?" she asks as she rings up the total.

"Not today, Janice," I reply dryly.

She reads off my total, and I pay the bill before taking my basket and leaving. When I get back to my car, I see that I have another text from Archie.

Archie: Do you want me to wait for you to go to the grocery store?

Me: No, you go ahead. I don't want to hold up your fun.

I'm grinning like an idiot as I pull out of the post office parking lot. Who said revenge isn't fun?

Chapter Seventeen

"You bought mint ice cream." I stare at the container on the counter as Archie unloads the groceries.

He's one of those people that empties everything out and groups things together before putting them away. Whereas I prefer to put it away as I go.

It's painful to watch.

"Where's the chocolate ice cream?" I ask.

He points to the mint. "Right there."

"That is not chocolate ice cream."

"It has chunks of chocolate in it!"

I look at him like he's the nail in my tire.

"I needed chocolate ice cream, crusher of dreams," I grind out.

He laughs like he's an adrenaline junkie looking for a near-death experience. His laughter stops abruptly when he sees the look on my face.

"Oh. Ohhh. I get it. Sorry. That time of the month. When I finish unloading this, I'll go back and get the chocolate ice cream."

His placating helps—a little.

"How did you get to the grocery store anyway?"

"Tripp picked me up. We grocery shopped together."

I'm surprised at the twinge of jealousy I feel at their bromance. "Does that man ever work?"

"Of course. It's just an odd schedule, working in the ER."

Okay, that makes sense.

"I'll go to the grocery store. Can't trust a man to get the right type of ice cream," I mutter to myself as I empty a bag of groceries. "If I send you again, you might come back with an abomination of ice cream. Something like cherry."

"You know it's still ice cream even if it's fruit-flavored," he teases.

"Nope. I refuse to believe it. It's a carton of lies, is what that is."

Archie sighs and grabs the keys off the counter where I set them. "Come on. Let's go back to the store. I'll go with you."

"I'll drive," I say as I reach for the key ring.

"I'm driving." He scrunches his eyebrows together and keeps the keys just out of my reach.

"I'll fight you for it."

He smirks and steps toward me. "Please do."

I swallow the lump in my throat, knowing that every joking wrestling match we've had in the past turned into something more.

"Right. You can drive." I head into the bedroom and kick off my jeans, then pull on my baggy sweatpants. I need all the stretch.

Archie doesn't say a word as we climb into the car, and he drives into town. It's a strange moment, though, since it's the first time he's driven since he's been back.

I have to bite my tongue several times to keep from screaming, but we make it to the grocery store without any major driving violations.

Archie follows me into the grocery store, and I take a little detour down the feminine products aisle. I pass him a box of tampons and another box of pads.

He doesn't say a word as I turn to march toward the ice cream aisle. I find a chocolate chunk brownie and pull it out.

"And that is what I mean when I say chocolate ice cream."

He holds the feminine products together over his head. "When can I come out of the doghouse?" He makes a whining sound, frowning with a sad look in his eye.

I will not smile. He starts whining louder in his tampon-constructed doghouse. Finally, I crack a smile.

"Are you all right?" someone asks from the end of the aisle.

It's a woman I recognize as one of Margaret's friends. She was there on bocce night, though I think she mainly stayed in the safety of the house. Another woman stops beside her. It's Esme from the library, who also works as a caregiver.

"It's okay, Clarice. His head's broken. He fell from the sky."

Clarice tsks loudly. "Why are the good-looking ones always the fallen angels?"

They continue walking past our aisle, and I have to

bite my lip to keep from bursting out laughing. Archie isn't as tactful. He cuts loose with a guffaw that would make a donkey proud.

"Did you hear that?" he whispers. His whispers are notoriously loud. Impossible to miss. "She thinks I've been kissed by heaven."

"And they also think you broke your head. I'm inclined to agree with them." I swap with him, handing him the frozen ice cream and taking the feminine products.

We hurry up to the cash register and speed back home.

There's ice cream that needs to be eaten.

Archie does the honor of grabbing two spoons and turning on the TV. We sit down next to each other.

"I forgot. It's Mom's birthday tomorrow night. We're invited by the family for dinner."

"Okay, that sounds great. What time? Do we have a present for her yet?" he asks.

"I bet Kingston already has it figured out. I'll text him and find out."

Archie fills my spoon and passes me a bite.

"Oh, no. Listen, bucko. You're the one who forgot about the ice cream. If you think you get to hang on to the carton, you're wrong." I snag the carton from him. "Should we watch a movie tonight? What do you want to watch?" I ask around a bite of ice cream.

"I don't know. Do we have a magnifying glass? Because we're going to need it if we want to watch anything on that screen."

We stayed up far too late, watching Sandra Bullock, my go-to woman for PMS, sadness, happiness, or any other mood I could possibly have. She's literally the answer to every problem, and she never fails to make me smile. Archie and I have different tastes on just about every-thing—clothes, food, decor, reading. But when it comes to movies, we actually like the same stuff. If it had been any other time of the month, I would have tortured him by telling him he loves reality TV, but then *I* would have been tortured by reality TV.

Morning hits hard, and I don't have an ounce of energy to go for a walk. Not to mention those cramps are kicking like an angry kangaroo. The best I can manage is stumbling into the bathroom and getting ready for the day.

I finish brushing my teeth, and just as I'm rubbing my face lotion in, I spot *it*.

Scary. Furry. Large. Teeth big enough to eat me. It's a spider that would like to make me lunch, scurrying across the ceiling above the bathtub.

So large that I can see its shadow as it runs.

"Archie!" I scream at the top of my lungs.

The spider pauses its sprint, and I press backward against the shower curtain.

"Archie!" I call again because I don't know if he's actually awake or not.

Archie bursts into the bathroom, yelling, "What's happening?"

I point at the *tarantula* in the corner of the bathroom.

Archie starts to laugh, slapping a hand against his jeans. How is he looking so chipper after such a late night? It's not fair that the man can function so well on a few measly hours of sleep. "That tiny thing? You've got to be kidding me."

I glower at him. "I'm not. Please kill it."

With a smirk, he grabs a magazine off the back of the toilet—don't judge me—and climbs onto the standalone bathtub, straddling the edges with both feet. He reaches up, ready to smite down my enemy...but he misses, and I watch in horror as the spider falls from the ceiling, spiraling down Archie's shirt.

We both scream like there's no tomorrow.

Archie frantically flings off his T-shirt as he jumps down, standing in the center of the tub.

"Where is it? Where is it?" I scream oh-so helpfully.

"It's in my pants!"

He's out of those in point-zero-two seconds, then he's out of the tub. Now, he's hopping around the bathroom in his briefs as we look for the giant.

It crawls out of his shirt that's been discarded in the bathtub.

"What do we do?" Archie yells as he looks around for another weapon.

"You were laughing at me!"

"I was wrong! It's the devil! Give me something to hit it with!"

I pass him my curling iron, but Gatsby beats us to it. He strolls into the bathroom and lazily leaps to the edge of the bathtub. He watches the spider scurry back and forth for a few seconds while his tail twitches. Then, he pounces. I can almost hear the crunch, and even though I wanted this outcome, the sound still makes me a little ill.

Gatsby picks up the spider in his mouth and carries it out of the bathtub. We follow him all the way to the back door, where he carries it outside.

"Phew. That was a close one," Archie says.

The cat door is still swinging, and we both stare at it as though the spider might make an escape and come back for us.

A knock sounds on the front door. We both shriek together.

"It's the spider mafia, coming to avenge its family."

Archie spins to stare at me. "What kind of books have you been reading?"

"I discovered audiobooks a few months ago. I had to sleep with a kitchen knife by the bed during my thriller kick."

"Are we going to find out who's at the door?" I ask. The curtains are still closed on the front windows, so it's impossible to see who it could be without looking through the peephole.

"Maybe they'll go away." Archie looks hopeful as he pulls me close to his bare chest.

The knock echoes loudly again.

"I'll answer it," Archie says as he reluctantly releases me and starts for the door.

"You're in your underwear!" I whisper.

He winks at me over his shoulder. "Maybe they'll realize we're busy."

He peeks through the peephole, then backtracks. "It's your brother. I don't want to be murdered today."

I don't mention to Archie that he's supposed to think we're married, because he's already in the bathroom, slipping back into his clothes.

I open the door.

"Hey, sis. I was just dropping by to get you to sign this birthday card." He shoves a card toward me.

"Is this your usual scam routine?" I tease, knowing it's a card for Mom.

Kingston is *the* gift guy. Oftentimes, he organizes a big gift for our parents' birthdays or Christmas. So, I know this is going to be good.

"What are we getting her this year?"

"We're sending Mom and Dad to Maui."

I nod slowly. "Good call. How much do I owe you?"

"I already paid for it."

"I figured that, but that's not what I'm asking. How much do I owe you for my part?" I take the pen and card he's still holding out to me like a determined car salesman.

"I had a bonus this year. I wanted to do something nice for them. All I need is your signature on that card, and they can go on their trip as a happy couple."

"I hate that you're the thoughtful one. Shouldn't I be the thoughtful one? I am the sister."

He grins. "Can't touch this."

"You're annoyingly cheerful tonight. What's going on?"

"I'm going on a date with Willa." He gives me a sheepish grin.

"That's nice." I finish writing a quick *happy birthday*

note to Mom. "Wait, my Willa? You can't have my Willa! I need her!"

"It's just a date, sis," he placates.

"No. No. No. No. You don't get to ruin a good thing I have going. You'll break her heart, and then she won't be able to look me in the eye since I'm your sister, and then where will I be? Friendless. PR-less. My business will be in the dumps, and you'll go on your merry way to break someone else's heart."

He rocks back on his heels.

"I should have known this was some warped olive branch." Smooth-talking little stinker just wanted to get my approval. In some warped part of my brain, I appreciate that he even bothered, but then I remind myself that he goes through dates the way I go through potato chips—*with gusto.*

"I thought you said I was a good gift giver." He shrugs his shoulders as though he's an innocent little puppy.

"You are, but you're horrible at interpersonal relations." I'm going to tell him off. Tell him to find someone else. To leave my friend alone.

"I've been told I'm quite good at them, actually..."

"Eww. Get out of here. And please, please don't ruin things for Willa and me." That sounded firm, didn't it?

He waves the card over his head as he walks back to his SUV. "Don't worry. It's nothing serious!"

"That's what I'm afraid of!"

I slam the door and turn around to find Archie standing in the living room, shirtless but at least wearing pants.

"What did Kingston want?"

I sigh and flip the lock on the door. "He had a birthday card for Mom. But I think he really just wanted to tell me he's taking Willa on a date this week."

"Is this a bad thing?"

"You know Kingston, so you tell me." I plant my hands on my hips and watch as Archie tries to keep a straight face.

"Willa runs your PR, right?"

We both turn to see a triumphant Gatsby walking in through the cat door, looking as though he just saved the world. I'm pretty sure there's a spider leg hanging from his mouth.

He's at least saved our world, so I guess he deserves to look smug.

"You met Willa at the bar," I remind him. "She's done wonders for my business."

"Then, this is a bad thing," he tells me.

His confirmation is what worries me. My fears are *not* unfounded. "I know. That's what I told him."

"Would it be fair to warn her?" Archie asks as he scoops up Gatsby, who begins purring as loud as a cheap department-store blender.

I'd be doing the same if I was pressed against Archie's naked chest.

"Meyer?" His amused tone has me snapping my eyes back up to his. "The date? Warning Willa? You kind of zoned out there a minute."

His smug look means he knows exactly what I was staring at. I pretend like nothing happened. "I don't know. He is my brother."

"It is your business, though."

"But family should always come before business." I'm grasping at a reason to not interfere.

"I would agree with that if it wasn't for a philandering Casanova of a brother."

He's not wrong. "Aren't you supposed to defend your sex?"

Archie shrugs. "Not if they're taking advantage of someone."

I open my mouth to blurt out the words *I love you* but manage to hold them in. I start choking and coughing. Archie sets down Gatsby and pounds on my back three times.

"That did not end well," he says with a laugh. "How about this? How about you feel out your friend Willa? See how she feels about your brother. See how she feels about dating in general. If she's a *white-dress-and-bouquet* kind of girl, maybe you could subtly enlighten her."

I nod slowly. "Good idea. That way, I won't be betraying anyone. Right?"

"Right."

We both nod slowly together. "Riiight."

I glance at the clock. It's already nine, and neither of us have had coffee. The clock is ticking on a caffeine headache, not to mention the cramps are coming back in full force.

As I make the pot of coffee, I add a couple extra scoops to combat my lack of sleep.

"What are we doing today?" Archie asks as he pulls out a dozen eggs and goes about making a pan of scrambled eggs.

I almost say I have to work all day. It's become habit

to try and avoid him. But I don't have to work all day, and I actually enjoyed his company last night. Maybe it wouldn't be the worst thing to see where the day takes us.

"I need to go to the post office today with some rush orders, but that's the only time-sensitive thing I have."

Archie stirs the eggs. "I'd like to go speak with the airplane mechanic. The towing company was able to get the plane out yesterday and take it over to the hangar. Margaret's friend said he'd take a look at it with me today."

Take him to the airport? Let him be around those death traps again?

"No flying, right?" The coffeemaker spits out the liquid gold, and it splashes in the bottom of the coffee pot.

"Right." He crosses his heart with the spatula.

"I'll drive you, then." I set out two mugs.

The pan clinks loudly when he sets it on the granite countertop. "Really?"

His suspicious look miiiight be warranted after the 'you love grocery shopping' thing, but I ignore it and fill our cups with coffee.

"Really. I have to admit I'm a little curious about what caused you to crash. I've always said airplanes can't be trusted." I push his cup toward him.

"Thank you." His fingers graze mine as he takes it from me.

I jerk my hand back, very aware that every nerve is firing off at the simplest touch. "I'll go grab the keys, then." My voice sounds like it hasn't been used in years.

Archie's lips tilt up in a knowing smile. Smug little...

"Why am I sweating?" I tug at the collar of my tank top. It still doesn't let enough air in.

"Because the sun is out?" Archie asks as he leads the way across the tarmac to a large green hangar.

"No, I think it's the airplanes."

Archie stops abruptly, and I slam into his back. He spins around and wraps me in his arms. He's solid. His arms surround me, and despite our closeness, I'm not hot anymore. My temperature regulates. My heart rate slows to match his. And I find myself wrapping my arms around his waist.

Archie runs a hand through my hair. "Meyer, you don't have to do this. You know I would never put you on a plane. And if being here is making you uncomfortable, I'd rather go home."

That wasn't what he said when we'd fought about him getting his pilot's license.

His gentle fingers playing with strands of my hair as I press my face against his chest ease my heart. "I'll stay," I mumble against his chest. I don't want to move. But the roar of an engine sounds, and I know I can't stay here all day. I lean back and look at him. "Hold my hand?"

A smile spreads across his face. "Gladly."

He grasps my hand in his, and we head toward the hangar once again. A small plane outside of the yellow is humming loudly and slowly rolling forward. Archie guides us out of its path and leads me into the large green hangar where a tangled-up heap of metal—his airplane— sits in the center.

A man walks around to the front of the plane and greets Archie with a handshake. I recognize him from Margaret's.

"Meyer, I'd like you to meet Lawrence. He's friends with Margaret."

The man smiles kindly at me and reaches out to shake my hand. "I've seen you around some but don't think I've ever met you."

"Nice to meet you." I shake his wrinkled, calloused hand and am impressed by the strength of his grip.

"I've got a refrigerator in my office with some drinks. Can I get you something?" He wipes some grease off the back of his hand onto his coveralls as he waits for my answer.

"Oh, no, thank you. I just finished a coffee."

"Well, help yourself in there. Now, I suppose you're here to take a look at your plane." He folds his arms across his chest and stares at Archie.

"I was hoping I could figure out what malfunctioned. I don't remember the accident."

I harrumph because of how specific he is speaking. Of course he doesn't remember the accident. But he does remember everything else.

Lawrence smiles briefly. "The National Transportation Safety Board called and wanted results right away. I think they just didn't want to send out their own mechanic. So, I already took a look at the old bird."

I really hope he doesn't talk about his wife that way.

Archie follows him to stand next to the engine compartment. "The chute didn't deploy?"

I've heard Archie ramble about this plane enough to

know that it has a parachute for the plane. I think it's brilliant. My question is, why don't all planes have that? Makes sense to me.

Lawrence answers him, "It did deploy, but it detached completely. We'll need to contact the company and notify them of the error. That's a big mistake."

"I'll say." I snort. Forget what I said about parachutes. You can't trust them. It's much better to stay on the ground.

Archie glances back at me with a wry smile.

Lawrence walks to the back of the plane. "I can tell you exactly what caused your wreck."

Me too. You were in the air when you should have been on the ground. But I keep my brilliant thoughts to myself.

"Wow. You're fast if you've already figured it out," Archie says. "What was it?"

Lawrence clears his throat. "You ran out of gas."

I cough.

Archie freezes.

And Lawrence just grins.

"I what?"

"You ran out of gas." The twinkle in his eye is definitely not my imagination. The mechanic is finding this incredibly funny.

Meanwhile, I'm trying to keep smoke from billowing out of my ears. *He ran out of gas.* Who does that? It's one thing to drive a car and coast into the gas station on fumes. But an *airplane*? That's what happens in war movies. Fuel tanks are shot out, and people parachute out of their planes. They do not simply 'run out of gas.'

Archie slowly turns to look at me. The sheepish grin on his face is not helping his cause.

"You crashed your plane..." I tap my foot against the concrete. The shaky fear is slowly replaced with rage. "Because you ran. Out. Of. Gas."

Archie wisely takes a step backward. Lawrence leans a hand against the side of the plane and watches the two of us with amusement.

"It would seem so."

"Gas! Archie!" I reach out and grab the nearest thing —a screwdriver sitting on a bench. I jab it at him, even though he stands more than four feet away. "You were flying in the air and forgot to fill up on gas."

Archie's eyebrows shoot up his forehead. "What are you going to do with that screwdriver?"

I glance down at it, then wave my arms through the air. "I don't know! Convince you never to fly again!"

I slam it back onto the bench I picked it up from, and Archie's shoulders relax.

He's wise enough not to try and touch me while I'm this mad. "Maybe you need a cold drink?"

Lawrence helpfully points to a man-door at the back of the hangar. "Fridge is back there."

I clench my fists and trudge back there because if I don't cool my temper, I may do something regrettable, like pick up a hammer next time.

Chapter Eighteen

After the morning spent at the hangar and the afternoon mailing my rush orders, Archie and I are in the car on the way to my parents' house for my mom's birthday dinner. My temper has cooled some...but not completely. I now feel zero remorse about forcing Archie to admit the truth. *He could have been killed.*

I'll need Kingston's help tonight.

We pull into my parents' driveway, and I see that Kingston is already here, along with another car that I don't recognize and Bailey's minivan with its trail of cracker crumbs.

"Ready for this?"

It's the first time I've seen Archie look unsure since he's been here. But now, he's walking into the house as a man who remembers.

Before, his confidence was the confidence of a man who knew that he belonged to the family. Now, he's faking. I still haven't decided how long I'm going to let this charade continue.

Archie nods slowly. "Let's do this."

We go inside, and I prepare myself for any kind of drama.

The top options I've thought of are: one, my mother yelling at Archie, and two, my mother yelling at me.

My mother is not even a yeller, but this might be the thing that pushes her over the edge—me showing up to her birthday with my ex-husband on my arm. Oh, and then there's option three: my dad might want to punch him.

As I frantically run through all the variations of each scenario in my mind, I realize that Archie's holding the door open for me, smiling at me knowingly.

We go inside, and I realize my fears were for nothing. Mom and Dad greet Archie with big hugs.

"Whose car is that out there?" I ask Bailey as I wait for Mom to let Archie come up for air.

Bailey tilts her head toward the living room.

Dr. Tripp Sharpe stands next to my mom's picture wall, hands in his pockets and looking unsure about the family gathering.

"Dan knows him through the hospital, so of course he and Mom have been inviting him to everything. He finally came tonight," Bailey explains.

Mom and Dan like to pick up strays. Someone looks lonely? Bring them home. Someone's new to town? Make them feel welcome. They're the extroverts every introvert didn't know they needed.

I watch as Archie nods to Tripp, and we all move into the living room to make small talk and watch Mom open her presents.

Besides Kingston glaring occasionally at Archie, everyone acts as if this were the most normal thing.

The kids are excited and drag Uncle Archie into the living room, where they've built a city out of blocks. He's immediately put in charge of the fire station.

I sit down on the couch next to Mom, who looks slightly teary-eyed as she watches Archie chase after Lily and Elijah with a fire truck. Leo toddles after him, laughing.

"How are you holding up, sweetie?" Mom whispers in my ear when Dad turns to talk with Dan and Bailey.

Kingston sits in the corner, alternating between staring at his phone and glaring at Archie.

"We're doing good," I answer, and I'm surprised to realize that I mean it.

Eventually, Kingston's glaring gets to the point where I suggest that we go get plates together to dish up the fancy pizza. Because apparently, we are all still fifteen and couldn't even get our act together to take Mom out to dinner or even bother to cook her a nice birthday dinner.

But she's been smiling happily, so at least the gift of our presence is enough.

"Oh, I think you've got it," Kingston replies when I ask for his help.

Marching over to his chair, I grab the back of his T-shirt and say, "Let's go make dinner."

He stumbles out of the chair as I jerk him towards the kitchen. I appreciate him playing along, since I don't think I could lift even half of him.

Tripp and Archie both stand up and immediately

offer to help. Archie glares at Tripp, but before he can say anything, the kids drag him off to the castle again.

I tell Tripp to sit down and enjoy himself since he's a guest, then continue pulling Kingston into the kitchen.

He frowns at me, but I drag him into the kitchen and spin him around to face me. "Stop being a butthead."

"What are you, twelve?" he snaps back.

"I was speaking in terms that you would understand." I spin around and pull the paper plates out of the cupboard and set them next to the pizza boxes.

"How can I not be mad at him?" Kingston flips open the pizza boxes, rearranging them so there's room on the counter for drinks.

"You don't see me being mad at him, do you?" I mutter as I pull out a pitcher to mix some lemonade.

"You should be, Meyer." He shakes his head angrily, tossing me the lemon juice from the fridge. "He left you."

"I did some pretty dumb things, too, remember?"

"He'll forever be the dumbass who walked out on you." He folds his arms across his chest as he watches me stir the lemonade.

I whisper angrily, "I told him to go!"

I gasp because I realize the truth has now been let out. Me screaming at Archie to just leave me in peace is not something I've ever admitted.

Kingston slowly unfolds his arms and stares at me. "You told him to go?"

"I told you all that I was not innocent in this fight," I reply defensively. I did.

When I spilled half my guts to Kingston after the divorce, I did have the maturity to say that I was guilty of things in our marriage and that it wasn't only one-sided. The problem was that I didn't say that I was the one who had finally snapped and told him to leave.

Kingston hooks a thumb through his belt loop. "When you said you were guilty of fighting with him or causing problems, I assumed it meant you folded his socks the wrong way just to irritate him. Meyer, you never do anything wrong. You never fight—except with me, of course."

"I appreciate the vote of confidence, but I can ruffle some feathers when I set my mind to it. I said hurtful things, and I regret it."

"But he doesn't remember. So, what are you gonna do?"

"That's just it, Kingston." I smile conspiratorially as I finish mixing the lemonade. "He does remember. And I need your help."

He glances sharply over his shoulder toward the living room and lowers his voice. "What do you mean, he remembers?"

"A few nights ago, he hit his head. That thunderstorm night. The next morning, I overheard him on the phone, telling his mom that his memories all came back after that hit. So, being a good snoop when I want to be, I stood outside the door and listened to his conversation. And I realized that he remembers everything—the divorce, all of it. But he told his mom that he wanted to keep pretending."

Kingston is leaning forward intently now. He looks as if he would clutch his pearls if he had any. Instead, he picks up a piece of pizza and shoves it in his mouth.

So, I continue in a whisper, "Apparently, he was flying that plane because he was on his way to see me. He was coming to apologize and ask for a second chance."

"Wait, so you guys have decided to get back together?"

"That's just it. He doesn't know that *I* know that he remembers. And as long as he's not going to tell me the truth, I've decided it's fine to have a little bit of fun with it."

I lean back from our huddle and fold my arms as I wait for the information to sink in. Just as I knew it would, Kingston's face lights up with a positively evil smile.

"You could definitely have some fun with this."

"Oh, I know, but I was thinking that I need your help with a little something."

We bring our heads together and whisper furiously for one more minute, and then with a bunch of giggles, we get busy setting the table for the pizza.

When it's time to call everyone for dinner, I realize Archie and Tripp are nowhere to be seen.

"I think they're on the back deck," Dad tells me.

I walk down the hall and find the sliding door open to the back deck. Voices filter out to me.

"That's my wife you've been flirting with," Archie is saying in a sharp voice.

"Really? You're going to be jealous when all I'm doing is trying to help you?" Tripp replies in a dry voice.

My penchant for eavesdropping has grown in the last week. I'm adding it to my list of important life skills from now on. I learn so many valuable things...

"All I see is you jumping to attention anytime she speaks."

"If I wasn't rooting for you guys, I wouldn't be telling her to stick it out with you."

"You've talked to her about us?" Now Archie sounds angry.

Tripp sounds bored as he replies, "Why do you think you're still in Oregon? I bought you that time. *I* told her the shock would be too much for you. *I* told her you needed the reality you were used to. *I* told her to keep your phone from you."

I rest a hand on the wall. That dirty doc, manipulating patients...

"Listen, I knew you were coming up to try and win her back. What kind of friend would I be if I didn't try to help you?"

They're friends?

"I'm not sure that was the kind of help I needed," Archie snorts.

"You're still here, aren't you?"

"Yes, but I haven't told her I remember everything yet."

"If I were you, I wouldn't wait too long to tell her. She obviously cares for you, otherwise you wouldn't be here," Tripp says.

I hate that he's right.

"I know. I'm just scared of the reaction." Archie sighs.

I really need to stop listening. I have enough information to unpack for the next three years. I carefully tiptoe back into the hall and slam the bathroom door, then thump loudly toward the sliding door once again.

I slide the door open with a bang. "Dinnertime!" I call out as though I haven't been standing there for the last five minutes.

Both of them turn to look at me, and Archie smiles. "We're coming."

I grip the handle on the door and force a smile on my face, as though I'm not contemplating locking those two conniving men outside.

We spend the rest of the evening telling Mom how brilliant and wonderful she is.

It's not a lie. She really is brilliant as a lead architect in her firm. And she truly is wonderful as a mother, who has put so much time and love into us kids and still does, even now while we're all adults.

She's looking at Archie like he's a long-lost son come home.

Archie joins in the fun of telling her what a great mom she is and the million ways she's wonderful. This is my mom's bread and butter. Words of affirmation is her love language, and she continually poured that into us growing up.

Tripp thanks my mom for being so welcoming of a stranger, and I can see the moment he's permanently etched himself into my family. Mom will never let him go now. He'll probably be at every holiday from here on out.

After dinner, Kingston, Tripp, Archie, and I clear the dishes, aka stuff the recycling bin full and wash the glasses and salad bowl. Bailey and Dan leave with crying kids in tow who keep insisting that they are not tired.

Tripp says his goodbyes and leaves the same time as

Bailey and Dan. An early shift at the hospital awaits him in the morning.

After the door closes after Tripp, I meet Kingston's eye and give him an exaggerated wink.

"Don't you think it's time to go?" Kingston says loudly. "We all know that Mom and Dad go to bed early." My parents' early bedtime fits perfectly with our not-so-evil plan tonight.

"Oh, yes, it is getting late," I reply with a sad sigh. "Late for Mom and Dad, that is. I'll just finish the last of the dishes real quick."

Archie's looking at us suspiciously, so he knows we're up to something.

I will admit nothing. He could torture me and not pry out my secrets. Okay, well, maybe, if he deprived me of coffee, then I would spill everything I know and don't know to him.

"It would be a shame to end the evening so early, wouldn't it?" Kingston says. "Besides, I know how much Archie loves line dancing."

Kingston drags out the word *love*, and if I wasn't fighting laughter so hard, I would hug him.

Archie walks up behind me and places his glass in the sink. His chest brushes against my back. He doesn't step back. Instead, he takes on a relaxed pose with his hands planted on the counter on either side of my hips. I can feel his coiled energy as he asks, "Line dancing? What's this about?"

His breath wafts over my cheek, and he presses closer.

My family—with the exception of Kingston—thinks

he's being sweet Archie, who believes we're still married. They don't know better.

They don't know that we're locked into a battle of wits. Or a battle with the hunk of man who's causing me to forget what I'm even doing ...

"Ouch!" The water I've been rinsing the glasses under has grown too warm for comfort.

"Uh-oh. Did you get hurt?" Archie's crooning voice has a hint of laughter tingeing it as he reaches past me to shut off the water. "Here, let me kiss it better."

I meet his burning eyes as he brings my hand up to his face, and he presses a deliberately sloppy kiss on the side of my hand. I yelp when his teeth nip at me.

Any guilt I might have felt about backing Archie into a figurative corner and forcing him to go line dancing? Yeah, that feeling is as gone as the good ol' days.

I reach for the kitchen towel. Archie grabs it at the same time. He keeps a firm grip on it as I dry my hands, almost as though he's afraid I might snap him with it.

"I hope you can dance in those shoes." I smile up at him.

"I was born for it," he grits out.

Chapter Nineteen

We make it to the bar at nine-fifteen. The DJ is announcing the start of another line dance.

Soon, someone is calling out the instructions to the electric slide.

Line-dance night is often sprinkled with swing dances in between. Archie likes the swing dancing but despises the line dancing.

"Oh, look. A herd of ducks waddling back and forth," Archie mutters to me.

When I turn to look at him in the eye, he's looking around with distaste, and it brings joy to my life.

"But you looooove line dancing."

His gaze sharpens when he finally looks at me. He grits his teeth before he answers, "Love it. Love it so much. So. Very. Very. Much."

My grin is dangerously close to being permanently imprinted on my face.

He leans toward me, his smile turning sinister.

"Archie, now, don't—"

"The cha-cha-cha is starting," Kingston says as he stops next to us, thankfully interrupting whatever Archie was about to say or do. I'm safe. *For now.*

We spend the next few minutes doing the cha-cha-cha and laughing every time I catch Archie glaring at me.

He gets payback when it switches to a swing dance, and he offers to be the example couple. He leads me through a series of spins and turns that leaves me wondering if I'm prone to vertigo.

After two more line dances, we pause to grab a drink from the bar. Archie orders both of us a virgin margarita, and I can't help but appreciate that he isn't drinking either. Kingston is now nowhere to be found, but I spot another familiar face coming through the crowd.

"Hey!" Willa smiles at me and greets me with a hug. "I didn't know you liked to come to Western Wednesdays!"

"Oh, Archie didn't want to miss out on it."

A warm hand settles on my waist, and I realize he's fighting my lies with physical proximity—hence the swing dance where I was glued to his front any time he could make it happen.

He's winning our little war tonight.

Every time he touches me, my brain short-circuits, and I have the overwhelming urge to turn around and climb into his arms.

"Who are you here with?" I ask her.

"Oh, just a couple of friends." And then her eyes land on my brother, who has resurfaced and is making his way toward her.

"Willa," he greets her warmly.

"Kingston." She smiles back.

Gag me now. I do not need to watch my PR manager and brother make lover eyes at each other. *Nope, nope, nope.*

On my top-ten list of things I'd like never to witness; it ranks right up there with finding out what hot dogs are really made of.

"Are you free Friday?" Kingston asks Willa as he shifts closer. *Ew, gross.* I don't want to watch my brother hit on someone.

My gagging isn't internal, apparently, because Archie leans his head down to bury his face in my neck, laughing along with me.

Feeling him there makes it nearly impossible for me to pay attention to Willa and Kingston's conversation, which I need to do. Their relationship—or lack thereof—will affect me directly. But all I can think about is Archie's warm breath on my neck and the shiver running up my spine.

"Do you think you'll have time between Thursday and Saturday?" she asks sweetly.

My brother doesn't answer right away, which makes me think that something might be wrong.

I push Archie away as I glance at Kingston. His expression drops at Willa's words.

His jaw is clenched as he grinds out, "It depends on if your hearing is good enough or not."

That's when I see the ice in Willa's eyes. "Well, I know some of us are just meant to be a good time and nothing more, so as long as you're okay with being a good time and nothing more as well, then Friday works great for me. Although, I do have another date at eight p.m. that night, so we'll have to finish before then, of course. But I've heard you're a little quick anyway."

Kingston glares at her and then turns and walks away without uttering another word.

I slow-clap for her because she deserves a standing ovation.

Willa shakes her head. "I'm sorry. I know he's your brother. And when he asked me out, I was really excited, but then I just overheard a conversation between him and one of his friends. Apparently, I'm just someone to fill the time."

I loop my arm through hers and look at Archie for help. I don't think I've ever seen Willa look mopey, so she must have fallen hard and fast for my asshole of a brother.

"Listen, I love my brother, but I have literally never seen him get his ass handed to him in a conversation, and I think that deserves a celebration."

Archie holds out his hand to Willa and waits for her to tentatively grab it. He tucks it under his arm, and we lead her toward the dance floor.

"This calls for a celebratory line dance, don't you think, honey?" Archie says over the top of Willa's head.

He *knows* I hate being called honey. This is a declaration of war of a new variety.

I smile back at him. "Of course, snookums."

Willa throws back her head and laughs. "You two are the best together. I can't believe I've missed out on getting to know you two together."

Before I have time to unpack that comment—or even shush her—Archie is tipping his imaginary hat to me and getting ready for his first line dance of the night.

Archie can do a lot of things. He can draw, he can fly —although after recent events, that one might be up for debate—he can sing, he can kiss. But the man cannot dance. And I mean, it's a *knock-over-everyone-in-the-vicinity* type of not being able to dance.

Willa thought I dragged her to the dance floor in between us just to cheer her up? She's wrong. I stuck her between Archie and me in an act of self-preservation. But halfway through the song, I realize it's not enough. Willa is doubled over with laughter, and I'm being tripped by a size-thirteen shoe.

He's switched places, and he's back to fighting with close combat. I'm pretty sure I'm losing.

Archie drives us home, and I'm grateful because, while I had fun line dancing, I also danced my little heart out. It's the lightest I've felt in ages—and also the most exhausted I've felt in ages.

Archie's constant barrage of touches hyped me up. Dancing every dance exhausted me. Now, I feel stuck in an exhausted, suspended state of emotional and physical anticipation.

I give up and close my eyes. In no time at all, someone is lifting me out of the car.

"You know, this is becoming a habit," I whisper sleepily against Archie's chest.

"I know. And it's a nice habit," he murmurs back. His

arms are firmly wrapped around me as he carries me up the sidewalk to our home.

This time, he's prepared with the key to the house, and he sets me down only briefly as he opens the front door.

He scoops me back up and carries me inside.

"Did you have fun? I'm sorry I made you line dance." My words aren't coming out very clear, and I think it's because I'm so tired. My lack of naps is starting to show.

"I always have fun with you, Meyer. Don't ever doubt that. Even when you are a pickle. Or maybe especially when you're a pickle," he teases lightly as he lays me down on my bed.

"I love dancing," I whisper as he pulls off my tennis shoes and socks. He rummages around in the dresser and pulls out a pair of jammies.

"This is becoming a habit, too." He lays the pajamas next to me.

His fist presses down on the bed as he leans over me. The weight on the mattress causes me to roll toward him.

"Are you going to kiss me good night?" I ask slowly. My hand fists in his button-up shirt.

He leans down to hear my words. "What was that?"

"I said, are you going to kiss me good night?"

Archie shakes his head, his nose brushing against my cheek. A shiver runs up my spine as he whispers in my ear, "The next time I kiss you good night, it's going to be a proper, thorough good-night kiss, and it's not going to stop at that."

With that, he leaves the room, and suddenly, I'm wide awake.

Chapter Twenty

Sleep eluded me. And I have only one person to blame.

Archibald Dunmore.

I pull on my shorts, because it's spring in Oregon, and there might be a small chance of sun and a high chance of irritating my husband.

I roll the hem up just a little higher, then pull a crop top from the drawer.

Yep, it's gonna be a good day to torture him. I do a full face of makeup, even fix my hair, and straighten my bangs so that they hang where they're supposed to.

When I walk into the kitchen, I can feel Archie's eyes boring a hole into me from where he's sitting at the table, sipping coffee.

"Were you planning on going swimming in that outfit?" he asks mildly as his gaze sweeps up and down my body. He points over his shoulder.

I glance out the kitchen window then mumble some not nice words.

My brilliant shorts outfit is completely ruined by the

temperamental Oregon weather. There's practically a monsoon outside. I set the coffee cup down with a snick and turn around to go change. This time, I come out wearing my faux leather pants and sweater crop top. I pick up my mug again and glance outside.

The rain has stopped, and the sun is shining brightly.

Archie wisely keeps his comments to himself, probably realizing that it's best to let me caffeinate before he tears apart any more of my ego.

He didn't kiss me good night, and I couldn't help but run through a list of reasons why.

Reason 1: I didn't brush my teeth after eating pizza.

Reason 2: He's not attracted to me anymore.

Reason 3: He wants to crush my hopes and dreams.

I pour the coffee into the cup and turn around to study the man who's busy drawing while sipping his coffee.

"I think I'm going to become an airplane mechanic," he says in a matter-of-fact tone, as though he said he was going to drink peppermint tea today instead of chamomile.

Just like that.

"And where do you learn to be an airplane mechanic?" *The Wright Brothers School probably.*

"There's a flight school here. In town. You've already met the instructor. And I just learned that Clarice is his wife."

"Clarice?"

"She was at Margaret's. She was also at the grocery store when we were buying tampons."

"Did she rob the cradle?"

"No, he's older than her."

"So, he's about forty years past retiring age," I guess.

"He says he's just now starting to slow down. His wife has the beginning stages of dementia, and he wants to spend more time with her while he can," Archie replies. "He's incredibly knowledgeable and reputable. I've learned a lot just from talking with him so far. The guy is practically a legend among pilots, and so if I were to learn from anyone, I'd want to learn from him."

"Will you have to fly any of these planes?" I ask with a catch in my throat.

"Maybe." He shrugs. "Mostly, I'll be working on the engines on the ground."

Apparently, I don't look appeased enough because he continues explaining, "Maybe on a ladder, but definitely not while I'm flying."

"Yes, Archie, I picked up on that. I'm just worried about you."

He sets down his pencil and his mug, folding his hands as he studies me. "Meyer, I love that you care enough to worry about me. But have you ever had something that you had to do? Like you knew you would love it so much? That you knew you'd found your thing?"

I nod slowly and whisper, "Yes."

"That's how this feels. It's like my missing puzzle piece. I'll be able to freelance graphic design on the side, all while working on planes."

I press a thumb against my forehead. It's scary that I'm not even surprised by this.

"I'm excited about it," he says quietly, as though he's waiting for my approval.

He doesn't need my approval. We're not married anymore. And he still cares what I think.

"I know what it feels like to get excited about something," I finally whisper.

Tripp stopped by to pick up Archie. The two of them seemed as bad as two middle schoolers going out together. Instead of a hike, they were going kayaking on the lake. Luckily, there is no gas required for that activity, and I made them promise to wear life jackets. (I'm not fooling myself; they probably won't. But it put my mind at ease to hear them say they would.)

After getting that reassurance, I disappear into my office to get some work done without any distractions.

I pull out a paper and pen, then stare at them. I'm caught up on my orders. I could be taking a nap right now, but instead, I'm thinking of a list of reasons why I don't want to take the Blanchett deal.

I've tried to come up with enough reasons that would seem plausible to an achiever like Willa, but I have nothing.

My top reason—I've even written it down—is that I like to nap.

There's no time for naps if you're supplying a chain.

I don't think Willa would appreciate that one. It doesn't exactly scream "capable, strong woman" if I simply don't want to do more.

I like my business. I like what I do.

And since I'm being painfully honest with myself, I

know that I could be perfectly happy just like this. Forever.

A fulfilling job.

A bungalow that I will *not* be selling—that wild-haired idea is officially gone from my mind.

A husband who I think might want me sometimes.

I definitely need to figure out that last one, but one challenge at a time.

I crumple the piece of paper and toss it in the trash. I can't present that to Willa.

Groaning in frustration, I plug in the glue gun and pull out my drawer of white buttons.

If I took the deal, I'd have to hire someone else to help with production. I'd prefer to keep it just me. I don't want to be someone else's boss.

Too much stress.

Why couldn't Willa be a little less of an over-achiever? The woman shot for the moon and hit it, bless her heart. It makes it even harder to say no to this because she's only doing her job. Expanding my business.

Maybe I should just do it.

I start making earring set after earring set. I work until I'm out of hot glue, then I unplug the gun, staring around the room. Where would my potential employees sit? I could maybe fit one more in here, but it would be cramped quarters. Where would they take their lunch breaks? How will I take my afternoon naps?

I'm sweating, just thinking about it.

I fold my arms onto the desk and rest my head while I wait for the glue gun to cool down completely before putting it away.

Just five minutes.

Chapter Twenty-One

My ringing phone wakes me up from my impromptu nap.

Disoriented, I check the name on the screen before I answer. You can't answer every phone call that wakes you up from a nap. It sets an unhealthy precedent.

It's Mom. That's an acceptable person to answer for.

"Hello?" I rub at my eyes and yawn.

"Hi, sweetie, I just was calling to thank you for that nice birthday present. I can't wait to go on that trip!"

"You're welcome. It was Kingston's idea." My mouth is fuzzy. I've probably been snoring in here.

Mom sighs. "Don't downplay your part. You know I love having you all over at the house together. It doesn't happen enough anymore."

Guilty. We really should make more of an effort where Mom and Dad are concerned. I make a mental note to text my siblings about it later.

Mom continues, "And it was nice to have Archie there, wasn't it?"

I sort through the small basket of buttons on the desk,

arranging them by size. I dig to the bottom of the basket, and my fingers bump against something familiar—the avocado keychain.

I slowly pull it out as my mom continues telling me how much she'd like regular family dinners to happen. I stare at the avocado. It's frozen, smiling face smiles back. Archie's been in here when I wasn't paying attention.

And he's laying his cards on the table, so to speak.

"Do you think Archie is doing okay? It was so good to have him there last night, even if he doesn't remember. Wouldn't it be great if he never remembered? You could just keep going forward the way you are!"

My mother the optimist. And the non-confrontationalist. We are too similar sometimes. I clear my throat. "I thought of that, Mom. But then I thought, what would he do when he remembers and finds out I've been tricking him? Besides, none of that matters anymore. His memory came back."

"It did?" she asks brightly. "When did that happen?"

I tell her about the stormy night that brought back Archie's memory.

"Neither of you said anything last night!"

"He hasn't said anything to me yet," I admit. I flip the avocado up in the air.

"Do you mean to tell me that he's pretending? Are you sure he actually remembers everything?"

"Yes, Mom, I overheard the whole phone call." I miss catching the avocado, and it falls to the ground. Gatsby pushes open the office door and wanders in to stare at me.

"What are you going to do?" my mom asks. Not

necessarily what I need. I need her to *tell* me what to do. I don't want to figure it out myself.

"So far, nothing." I bend down and scoop up the keychain, then walk to my room and set it in the night-stand drawer.

"He wants to be with you," Mom says smugly.

"How do you know that?" I ask as I shoo Gatsby out of my room. I trip over a pair of Archie's shoes in the hall-way. He never can seem to put them where they go.

"The way he looked at you last night. I was sure he didn't remember."

I freeze in the middle of the laundry room. "What do you mean?"

"I mean that he looked like he was in love." Mom's voice fades in and out as though she's busy cleaning something as she talks with me. It's impossible for her to make a phone call and not start absentmindedly cleaning something.

"Oh, your dad's calling. I've got to run. Love you!" She hangs up before I can say anything, and I'm left staring at my back door.

"Shall we, Gatsby?" I slip on my gardening crocs and open the back door for us.

Time to do some yard maintenance. If you can't solve your problems by thinking about them, then it's time to do something different.

"What am I going to do?" I ask Gatsby as we pull weeds in the back flower bed. "Should I tell him I know? Should I apologize?"

Gatsby licks his paw. "Or should I wait for him to

grovel? He didn't exactly run out of here screaming when his memories came back."

Gatsby moves on to the other paw.

"Or maybe I should kick him out. That would teach him."

"Yes, it would."

I jerk my head up and stare at Gatsby. He's no longer licking his paws. He's sitting there, staring right into my soul. "What did you say?"

"I said, 'yes it would.'" The voice comes from behind me, *thankfully*. My cat has not recently learned to talk. Although, that wouldn't be the most surprising thing he's done.

Margaret is standing in my backyard, holding a casserole dish. "I knocked, but no one answered. That husband of yours must not be home."

"Ex," I say automatically, without feeling.

"Well, I brought you my special casserole. It has the secret ingredient in it."

I'm scared to ask. "It smells great."

"You can pretend like you made it, and he'll fall in love with you all over again." Margaret is always so helpful in her suggestions. I go back to weeding as I realize she's here to gossip more than to deliver a casserole.

"Pretty sure that ship has sailed." I jerk a large thistle from beside my lavender plant.

"You mean that plane has taken flight?" She chuckles.

I frown as I toss the weed aside. "More like crashed."

Margaret shakes her head. "I know you two will make it. But you might need some help from me."

I shudder to think of the day that I'll need Margaret to help me repair a relationship.

"You forget that I've known you your whole life," Margaret says in an uncharacteristically soft voice. I glance at her, leaving my pesky weed where it is.

"A lot of people have." I don't know why I'm being so snippy to her. It's Margaret. She's always butting into everyone's business.

But then I really look at her. And I see the kindness in her eyes. She's standing in my yard with a casserole when Archie is not home. Which means she's here to check on my well-being.

My eyes mist over. "I think my heart's going to get broken again."

Margaret shuffles over and shifts the casserole dish to one hand. She reaches out a thin hand and pats me firmly on the shoulder. "There, there."

I think I'm going to have a bruise. Physical comfort has never been her strength.

"I happen to be fairly observant, despite my advanced years."

I laugh at that and swipe at a stray tear.

"He came back for a reason. And I'm positive you two will work it out. I'm sure you won't disappoint me. A second time." She raises one eyebrow at me.

"Someone was bound to break your perfect record...it just happened to be us." Margaret has played piano at nearly every wedding in town. It's become a bit of local legend that if Margaret plays at your wedding, then you'll have a long and happy marriage. Archie and I were the first divorce to break her record. I'm not completely sure she's invested in seeing us get back together for the right reasons.

"I just want you to know I'm here for you two. It's only a matter of time before you both come to your senses. So, I'll go set this in the kitchen for you." She marches into the house without another word. "It's coffee cake, not a casserole by the way."

"Thanks for the warning," I snap at Gatsby as I gather my weeds to throw in the yard debris bin.

I find myself hoping that Archie will be home soon—hoping that Margaret is right. *Someone* needs to come to their senses soon.

Chapter Twenty-Two

"What are you drawing?" I rest a hand on the table and lean over to see what Archie's sketching.

He returned from kayaking with Tripp all in one piece, plus some windburned cheeks. He's been sitting here sketching while I wash the casserole dish that Margaret brought over last night.

I slip the avocado into the bottom of his pencil bag while he's distracted, busy explaining what he's working on.

It's not an illustration so much as a portrait of us. Archie and I are walking along the trail, hand in hand, next to Green Lake. He's gazing down at me with a wistful look on his face. And I'm smiling warmly back at him.

A second breath, and I turn to look at Archie.

"Is this how you see us?"

"This is how I hope we could be," he says softly.

"Do you think it's possible?"

"With enough time," he replies honestly.

It's the best thing he could've said to me in that moment. Because I want the same thing. But I'm not sure I can do that right now.

Too much hurt, too much time, too much change. I want to know how much Archie has changed over the last year as well. Because I know I have. I hope I changed for the better, because if Archie is coming back to have the same relationship, then he won't find it here.

I've grown. I've changed. I've learned to stand on my own two feet. Or I should say, I am learning to stand on my own two feet. I'm learning the importance of *no* and the power it has.

Archie clasps his hands together over the pencil as he looks me dead in the eye. "I know I've hurt you. But I want a chance at us again. A chance to be happy together."

I wait for him to admit the truth, but he's staring at the picture again, lost in thought.

"I think we've changed. The years have taken their toll on us. I know I don't want to continue being separated from you. This fight, this thing between us...we can fix it."

He hasn't admitted to remembering, and his words are vague enough that I can't be sure if calling him out on it right now would be a good choice or not.

So, I hold my tongue and stare at the paper with him.

Archie finally breaks the silence and changes the subject. "I'm going to meet with Stanley, the mechanic, today."

I look at him sharply. "So, you're serious about this?"

He nods slowly. "I've always been interested in

airplanes. This seems like a practical way to enjoy that interest. But I wanted to keep you informed."

"Are you sure you don't have anything else you'd like to tell me?" I set my coffee cup down on the table with a loud thump, and I rest my hands on the center of the table as I lean forward.

Archie stands up slowly, his chair scraping across the floor. He braces his hands on the center of the table and presses forward until our noses are almost touching.

"What would you like me to say?" His voice is husky, and I hate that it's making me forget to be mad.

"Oh, I just wasn't sure if there was something you'd like to get off your chest."

"If you want me to take my shirt off, you can just ask." His teeth sink into his bottom lip as he fights a grin.

I reach forward and fist his T-shirt, tugging him closer.

Our noses are definitely touching now.

"I'm done playing games, Archie. If you want something—" I should force him to confess.

But before I have the good sense to stop myself, I'm kissing him. I'm taking those warm lips with mine. I press my hand against his chest, and his rapid heartbeat thumps against my palm.

His hand comes up to the back of my neck, fisting my hair, kneading the sore muscles there. I groan as he tips his head to gain better access.

He's hanging onto me as he drags both of us to the end of the table. He slips around to the side and grasps my hips, tugging me close to him. "This. This is what I want," he whispers against my neck.

He bends down, lifting me with an arm around my waist, and I wrap my legs around his waist. He takes a few stumbling steps toward the living room before he pauses to find my lips again, backing us toward the couch.

I'm equally impatient. My hands tremble as I thread my fingers through his hair. Every whisper of a touch. Every flirtation. It's culminated to this. Me, happily losing all sense of time as I kiss my ex-husband.

"I can't believe I walked away from this," he mutters against my lips.

That has me pulling back. Taking a shaky breath, I finally open my eyes to stare into his.

Stark terror sits there.

Oh, right. I'm not supposed to know about him having his memory back.

I do my best to look shocked.

Chapter Twenty-Three

"You remember," I accuse. *Like I haven't known all along.*

Archie sets me back down on my feet, but he doesn't let me go. He cocks his eyebrow at me. "You knew already. Do you think I didn't catch on to you telling me 'new' things about myself? I knew you'd be mad at me, but I knew you wouldn't purposely do any long-term damage. I knew you would only do those things if I was already healed. Although, I am a little upset that the tiny TV really was my idea," he muses.

I take a step back so that the backs of my legs are pressed against the couch. "You were going to pretend like you still didn't remember our divorce!"

He shrugs sheepishly. "I didn't know how to broach the subject with you. We'd left things so badly. I just needed time to process my feelings, my memories, and to see how you felt about me." A small smile cracks across his face. "I wasn't disappointed."

I turn around and grab a cushion off *my* blue couch

and smack him upside the head with it. He jumps back, narrowly dodging the coffee table, as though he has all the time in the world.

"Jeez, you did get violent while I was gone."

I smack him again with the pillow. "How long were you going to pretend?"

Another smack to his shoulder.

"I didn't mean to hurt you!"

"You left me!"

"I meant right now. I'm not talking about the past. Not yet. I meant that I wasn't sure how to tell you the truth about me remembering without hurting you. I needed a couple days to sort out things in my mind. Everything seemed so jumbled together."

I stop smacking him with the pillow, realizing that he's probably telling the truth, which is unfortunate, because it's much easier to stay angry at a liar.

I hug the pillow to my chest and nod slowly. "Okay, you have a point. I will try to control myself. We will sit down on this lovely blue couch and discuss this like adults."

"It is a lovely blue couch," he taunts as he sits down.

I lift the pillow like I'm going to smack him again. He jerks it out of my hand and stuffs it under one of his legs.

He points at the cushion next to him. "Sit down."

"I don't want to."

"Your newfound voice is amazing. It's like every thought you've ever suppressed is now bubbling up at me."

He's not wrong. But just to be contrary, I flop onto the couch in defeat.

"You're a safe space for me to let out my anger." Admitting the truth doesn't make it better, but maybe now that I've said it, I'll be able to do something about it—like stop making Archie bear the brunt of my anger.

"I missed you, Meyer." He says it slowly, deeply as he looks me in the eye. "And that is directly from current Archie, not forgetful Archie."

"Do you remember why you came back?" I ask, wanting him to say it to me, not just for me to overhear it while he's on the phone.

He nods slowly. "I remember everything. I remember us. I remember everything leading up to that big fight. I remember that the big fight didn't have anything to do with this blue couch—not really. I just picked something to be obstinate about."

"And then I told you to leave," I say softly.

Archie looks at me in surprise as I shrug.

"We're past due to own up to our mistakes."

He taps his fingers against his kneecaps, and he echoes, "And then you told me to leave."

"We needed to do some growing up, didn't we?" I agree with him.

He sighs before he says, "I just wish that we'd grown up together rather than going through a divorce."

"What did you hope to accomplish by coming back?" I ask.

He rubs his palms together and stares at the floor. The mantel clock that I thought had run out of batteries ticks loudly while I wait for him to answer.

"I want to fix what I broke." He says it softly, brokenly.

"*We*, Archie. We both broke it."

"I wanted to come back to see if you still loved me. I wanted to see if there was any chance that we could repair what was broken, to have a second chance together."

"You mean to tell me that you got in a plane wreck while coming up here to have a second chance at a relationship with me?" My voice ends on a shrill note.

He smirks. "The irony is not lost on me, trust me."

"What about your work in Arizona?"

"My campaigns were all finished, and so I simply took a month off."

"Took a month off?" I ask incredulously. "How do you take an entire month off?"

"It's the schedule this company runs on. We were in between campaigns. I had been waiting for that moment to come. They didn't need me for anything."

"Do you remember crashing?" I ask because it's safer to talk about the tangible rather than us.

"No, actually," he says as he shakes his head. "All I remember is, it stalled out on me. Everything after that is gone. Makes me wonder if I'll ever remember the details."

"See?" I shout. "Planes cannot be trusted."

Archie shakes his head. "A distracted man cannot be trusted."

I open my mouth to argue, but I agree completely with him. "You ran out of gas. In an airplane. Gas! Archie!"

He gives me a playful scowl. "I'm paving the way for electric planes."

I rub a hand across my forehead. "Please don't scare me like that again."

His eyes sharpen on me. "Again? Does that mean you expect me to be around here?"

Do I?

❀

ONE YEAR, TWO MONTHS AGO: THE FIGHT

"We are not buying a blue couch!" Archie snaps at me. We stand in our living room, and he's pointing at our disgusting faded-red couch that looks like it escaped from a crime scene.

It was a hand-me-down to us from the people we bought our house from. My side hustle of selling button earrings has finally made it possible for me to buy my dream couch. The one that's been on my wish list for over a year now.

"It's robin-egg blue, and it's going to look great in our living room," I reply in the face of his anger. It's not as if he spends much time here anyway. He's been so busy at his finance office and then sketching at the lake, where he 'feels less stifled.'

"No! It's going to ruin the whole vibe of this house!" He presses his lips together in a hard line.

"You mean the rustic, chain-smoker, '70s vibe?" Pretty sure there's a pack of smokes still in that couch.

"A blue couch is not going to make me feel creative!"

"All you do is come home and fall asleep on that

couch. The only thing you're creating is sound waves when you snore." I fold my arms across my chest.

He glares at me. "Don't. You know I don't like my job."

"You told me that last week, as if it was my fault you hate finance! I didn't make you do that!"

"You wanted to buy this house!" He waves his arm around as though I demanded he buy me a mansion, rather than a small home in a modest community.

"It was a good deal. And excuse me, but I'm working full-time, too. There is no 'you' in this situation," I manage to ground out.

"You sell real estate for a living! You know that's different than finance. You don't have the same pressures that I do. It's different because you are successful at what you do."

I stare at him incredulously. "The same pressures? The same pressures? Every day, I'm tasked with finding people their dream homes! With arguing with every realtor and loan officer and homeowner! Not to mention banks and inspectors! You have no idea what I go through. If I want to come home and relax on a blue couch in the evening, then I'm going to do that!" I fold my arms across my chest.

"Well, you're not using my money to buy it."

I freeze. Not that I was moving much. I've been wrapping my arms around myself, hoping to disappear into a black hole somewhere. Now, I want to actively search for that black hole.

"Do you think of us that way?" I ask quietly. "As two separate entities?"

He sighs, suddenly looking tired beyond his years. I wonder if I look the same. It's been a hell of a year. "Don't you?" He asks. "When was the last time we were together on anything?"

I clench my teeth, willing myself not to sob. Because it's the truth. We've been apart. Our careers slowly pulled us under. In our desperation, we've poured ourselves into our hobbies, only separating us more. He doesn't understand that I hate my job. He chose finance. He went to college for it. He knew he was signing up for a high-paying, high-stress job. I became a real estate agent to help pay our way while he was a full-time student.

"No matter how much I encourage you in your job, it doesn't matter. You've still pulled back from me," Archie says.

I refuse to think about the tinge of hurt in his voice.

"You don't want to keep this house the way we found it. You want to change it! You painted that classic wood paneling while I was gone, and you didn't even care what I thought about it. You've made different changes, and you don't even care what I think."

"Why would I think you would care? You're at work, or zoned out on that couch, or busy on your tablet! You never bother to ask me what I want to do or spend time with me."

"All you care about is bubble-wrapping your world to keep it safe. You hate the idea of me flying!"

He recently expressed an interest in flying again. He has his pilot's license, and he talked about buying a small plane that he could use.

"You know I don't want you to die in a plane crash! I'm not being unreasonable!" I scream.

"Because you're so busy making this house a safe haven for *you* that you can't imagine someone wanting to do something different."

"Well, at least I want to be here! You never do!"

"Because you don't let me in anymore! You don't support me in what I want to do. I think I'm all done even trying!"

"Why don't you just leave, then?" I finally scream. The pain, the hurt, the grain of truth in his words are cutting through me. I want it to stop. I want this fight to stop. As soon as I say the words, I regret them.

They shock him—at first.

But then he slowly nods. "Okay, then. I'll give you what you want."

PRESENT DAY

"We were both idiots, weren't we?" I say. Thinking back over the things that led us to that place, it's easy to recognize two young kids who didn't know how to balance the pressure of careers and marriage. We withdrew, then snapped.

Archie nods emphatically as he reaches for my hand. "I wish I had given you some warning before I came flying up here. It seemed like a good idea at the time. I'd had an entire year to regret that I walked away."

"What gave you the courage to fly here with no warning?" I slip my hand into my pocket and find a spare button in there. I pull it out. A small pink one.

"Life was wrong without you." Archie takes the small button from my fingers. He runs his thumb back and forth across it. It's tiny in his hands. He keeps his attention on the button, and I hold my breath, waiting for him to explain himself.

"But without you there, I saw how much growing up I needed to do. How much I needed to own it myself. Funny how you can never outrun yourself."

"I might not have been the runner, but I buried it. I'm sorry I hurt you. How did you come to be out here? And does it have anything to do with Tripp?"

Archie fights a little smile. "I met Tripp through a colleague at work. We hit it off over our love for Oregon. I told him about Green Lake. He listened to me talk about the wife I left behind. Once a position came up at Green Valley General, he applied for it and got it. He was one of the first people I called to tell him I was coming back to see if there was any hope for us, to see if you still loved me the way I love you."

A small fissure cracks open the protective casing I've built around my heart.

"He knew about us the whole time?" All those "helpful tips" he gave me. Sneaky, little...

Archie nods slowly. "Please don't be mad at him. He was trying to do me a favor."

"I'm not sure if I should be furious or amazed. He's not exactly what I pictured cupid looking like." I smirk as I imagine Tripp playing the role of a matchmaking dowager in a historical romance... He'd look fantastic in a powdered wig.

"I'm scared to ask," Archie says with a grimace.

There are some things that are too difficult to explain. "Yeah, you probably should be."

We sit and stare at each other for a few more minutes.

"So, what are we gonna do about us?" he asks.

I take my time to respond, tracing the edges of the couch with my index finger. "Well, it would be a shame for you to have come all this way for nothing."

The bright look in his eyes can only be hope.

"But, Archie, it's going to be like starting again. There's so much water under the bridge."

"I don't know that I want to start again, because I think all those hard things that we've gone through together have made us who we are today."

I hate that his philosophical idea is right. I just want to start peacefully, to not fight through anything. I'd like him to pretend like we've never had a fight.

He's right. Our divorce is part of us. It's what pushed me to my darkest point and also forced me to own up to who I was as a person. In a way, it's brought about the best in me. And it's only fair to be that person with Archie now.

We've both done a lot of growing up. We've grown into the people we were meant to be rather than pushing each other into specific boxes—even on accident.

"What do we do first?" I ask.

A knock on the door interrupts whatever Archie is going to say.

Chapter Twenty-Four

"Maybe we can pretend we're not home," Archie suggests.

"I would agree, except they probably saw us through the window when they walked up the sidewalk."

Archie points a finger at me. "We are going to finish this conversation later."

I try to tame my bangs before I go to answer the door.

Willa stands on my front porch, wearing a big smile. "I know I didn't call or warn you, but I saw your car in the driveway. I had to stop by and tell you the best news! My uncle Robert from Blanchett emailed me the contract for the deal!"

Her squeal has Gatsby meowing back in the call of his people.

"Wow, I just—" I don't get to finish that thought because now, Archie is standing behind me, greeting Willa.

"Hey! How's it going, professional line dancer?" he greets her with a big smile.

"It's great! Did Meyer tell you everything? Oh, of course she did. I'm sorry. It's such a great thing. She'll be expanding her business with Blanchett. We'll probably have to start hiring because, otherwise, Meyer will have to work around the clock."

Willa is well caffeinated today. Someone needs to teach her about the dangers of energy drinks.

"Wow! Meyer, you mentioned it in passing. I didn't know it was such a big deal or that it went through!"

Willa waves a hand through the air. "Isn't that just like her? She's so nice to work with. Trust me, I work with some real a-holes who think they are God's precious gift to the world. Spoiler alert: they're not. And then I work with Meyer here, who is always bending over backward to not be a pain in the butt. I had to pour everything into this deal for her."

Willa's levitating, and I feel sick to my stomach.

Willa and Archie go back and forth excitedly, and all I want is to go lie on that couch and nap.

"Okay! I'll have it printed up and ready to sign in a couple days. Brunch as usual?"

I find myself smiling extra bright and agreeing. "Of course! That sounds wonderful, Willa. Thank you so much!"

She leaves, and I close the door in stunned silence. I guess a part of me was hoping the deal would fall through, that I wouldn't be backed into a corner like this. Leave it to Willa to actually make miracles happen.

Archie pulls me in for a hug. "Honey, I'm so proud of you! You've grown your business so much. It's becoming such a big deal. I'm so impressed by you!"

Impressed by an imposter. Hello, blinking neon light flashing off my forehead that reads *FAKER*.

Yep, that's what I am. A big, giant fake.

"You'll be hiring your own employees. You are the hashtag girl boss!"

I finally snap. "I don't want to be a girl boss! I want to make jewelry and take naps."

I turn around and grab my sweatshirt off the hook, slip into my tennis shoes, and run out the door. I leave everything behind, but at the moment, I don't care. I need a minute. One short minute to collect my thoughts. Why did everything have to happen in a day?

Why did Archie have to come back? Why did Willa have to push such a big deal at me?

Why can't people just leave me alone?

I need my own tropical island.

Ha. Joke's on me. I'd only be able to afford that tropical island if I take the deal that Willa has brokered.

Chapter Twenty-Five

The crunch on the trail has me glancing over my shoulder. Archie's picking his way toward me, a resigned look on his face.

"I'm sorry," I whisper.

He sits on the fallen log next to me, passing me my pepper spray for me to slip into my jeans pocket.

He slowly wraps an arm around my shoulders, tugging me into his side.

"I know you've had a lot today, and I wanted to give you space for a while. But I also want you to know that I'm here for you if you need me."

I open my mouth to say thank you, but he cuts me off.

"I want to support you, Meyer. I want to be excited about the things you're excited about. But I don't know how to do that if you don't tell me how. I can't always guess what you're thinking. I can't always guess what your hopes and dreams are. I want to be with you. I've never stopped loving you. But I'm going to need help to love you the way you need it. I'm not sure what I said or did back there to hurt you."

I take a long, shuddering breath and then sit up to face him. "There's stress hanging over me. A pressure to be what everyone else wants me to be. To grow my business. But I'm not that. I am not a corporate-ladder climber. I'm not someone who can let go of her first love. I can't be bold and tell people off. It's not in me to do that. I want everyone to be happy—Willa, my family, Kingston... you. And I think if I keep squashing my own desires, then I can keep the world spinning. That if I keep my dreams to myself, then I don't have to worry about hurting anyone else's."

"And what is your dream job?"

I whisper, "I'm doing it right now. I love it. I don't want it to change. I like it like this. I don't want to grow. I make a great income right now. And if Bailey has an emergency? She can call me during the day, and I'll go help her. Willa and I can have late brunches together and pretend it's for work. I can listen to audiobooks while I create. I'm living my dream job, Archie. I get to be creative while having a flexible schedule. I don't want to give that up. But I know, to everyone else, it looks like I'm settling."

His large hand starts rubbing circles on my back.

"You know what? Some people might look at it like that. Then again, they might not. But even if they do, I want someone else to stand up for me. I hate confrontation."

His hand squeezes my shoulder. "Listen, Meyer. I wish I could do it for you. And I could. I could tell everyone off for you, tell them what you want and don't want. But I think you've grown too much in the last year to let that happen. You've learned to stand on your own two feet when you didn't think you could. You've learned to defend yourself—physically, mentally, and emotionally.

"Now, it's time to connect that with your voice. You don't have to be a jerk who yells at everyone and demands her way. But if there's something you feel strongly about, you need to speak up. So many people love you and want the best for you, but we can't help you if we don't know what it is that you actually want. We're left guessing. Even after talking with you today, I'm not sure that you really want me back or if it just seems comfortable for you to not tell me to leave again."

I groan at that because it's scary how well he knows me and how I'm not sure what I really want. I really do need time to sort through it.

"I love you, Meyer. And I will always love you. But when we get back together, it's going to be because it's something that you want. It's not going to be because I pressure you into it. Because if we have a second chance, I want it to be for life. If we have fights again, we'll go to therapy or counseling or something. If we need a hobby to do together to keep us close, I will take piano lessons from Margaret."

I laugh at that, and Archie smiles wistfully.

"I don't know that we would survive that, but it's an option."

"I don't want you to forget me twice."

"Twice? I doubt I'll get amnesia twice."

"You left me and forgot about me. That's what I'm talking about. Amnesia made you remember me. I'm not sure I could handle going through everything another time."

"You need time, Meyer. I promise I won't forget you twice. But what I'm saying is, it's your turn to take charge of your life, Meyer. If you don't want that corporate deal, you've got to tell her. If you don't want me in your life, you've got to tell me. But you're going to have to step out of your comfort zone to get what you want."

I watch as he stands up from the log, brushing the dirt from his butt. "I want you to take time to think about what you really want, Meyer. Because I'm all in on this. But I'm not gonna crowd you on it. So...I'm going back to Arizona."

I suck in a short breath.

"You need time. A lot has happened in a few short weeks. And you need time without me pressuring you into anything. I want you to be sure of your decision. I want you to be sure of me. So, if you need me, I'm only a phone call away, and then I'll be jumping on a plane to come back to you."

The air is sucked from my lungs, and my chest aches as I fight to take a breath.

Archie stands there studying the lake. The light breeze kicks up a small puff of dust from the trail. A bird chirps in the distance, and the musty scent of the woods fills the air.

A fish jumps in the distance, a muted splashing sound audible all the way to me on my log.

Finally, he looks over his shoulder at me. "I love you, Meyer, and no matter what, that isn't going to change."

My heart cracks a little more as I realize I don't have the capacity to answer that declaration.

Instead, I walk back to the house with him, barely staying on the trail with my blurry eyes.

When we get back to the house, he immediately packs his things and goes to stand on the front porch until Tripp picks him up.

This heartbreak is exactly what I've been trying to avoid.

Chapter Twenty-Six

Over the next two days, I wallow like a professional wallower. I have zero creativity. No inspiration. I don't answer calls, texts, much less open a social media app. I go rogue. Just me and Sandra Bullock together. And years of memories and regrets.

The only sign that Archie's been here is the sketch of the two of us walking by the lake, hand in hand, sticking to the fridge.

But during my wallowing time, I realize two very important things.

One, I think I might be in love with my ex-husband.

Shocking, I know. But the truth is, I don't know that I ever fell completely *out* of love with him.

The second thing I realized—much less of a shock—is that I want to keep the business the way it is.

I can do something about number two, even if it's uncomfortable. So, I rehearse a million ways to explain things to Willa when we meet next.

When the time finally comes, my hands are shaking. I

walk into the restaurant and sit down. I'm there first, so I order us both coffees.

Willa walks through the door, leaving a wake of cheery greetings and ample head-turning as she makes her way to me. She sits down across from me and flops out the contract from her bag.

"Are we ready to make this official and send it back?" She takes a long sip of the coffee in front of her. "Thanks for getting me a coffee. I need all the caffeine I can get this week."

I swallow the lump in my throat and whisper, "No."

Willa's smile freezes on her face. "No? No caffeine?"

Shaking my head slowly, I reply, "Willa, I haven't been fair to you. I know that I should've spoken up sooner." I take a drink of the ice-cold water in front of me. Then, I take a sip of coffee because maybe more caffeine will counteract my shakes. "I like my business the way it is. And I know this is huge for you to land a deal with Blanchett. I don't want to negate that or downplay it, but I don't want to be a boss. I want to enjoy creating, making a living off of my jewelry, but I don't want to turn into an entrepreneur that only runs the business side of things. I'm a creator. That's the part I love."

Willa's smile is gone, and she's looking contemplative as she taps her red nails against the file.

"Please say something," I whisper.

"I'd be lying if I said I wasn't disappointed."

I flinch and prepare myself for a big tirade.

She sighs. "But honestly, I probably wanted this way more than you did. It feels like next-level for me. I was excited to be able to tell other clients that I had landed

Blanchett for you, that I could get big deals like that. I wanted it so bad that I didn't pause to read the room. I've noticed your lack of excitement, and I should have checked in with you on that."

"I worry that maybe I led you on by not making my intentions clear."

"No." Willa shakes her head. "I remember you clearly stating that you loved having a small business that you could do completely by yourself—and of course, with me," she adds with a smile. "But I kept pushing. So, that's on me."

"Yes, but I'm the one who hired you, so I should have been better at communicating what I wanted for my business," I admit.

She frowns. "I guess I won't be able to tell anyone about the Blanchett deal."

I sip my coffee as I stare at her. Besides her being let down, nothing horrendous has happened. She hasn't quit. She hasn't ended our friendship. Instead, she's sitting there, sipping coffee at the same pace I am.

This was highly unexpected. Although Willa has never lashed out at me before. Maybe I need to stop expecting the worst when I voice my opinion.

"You know, you can always say that you turned down the Blanchett deal. You hold the power in that."

Willa's eyes sparkle at me over her cup of coffee. "That does have potential. Their deal wasn't good enough for my client. *I* am the PR manager who gets to turn down big deals that aren't right for businesses."

We begin to go back and forth, trading fun ideas of

options for how she could spin this, talking about other business offers she could potentially turn down someday.

The rest of brunch is spent talking about low-key ways to market my business and increase my profit margin. It's the first deep breath I've had in a few weeks. And it isn't because someone else fixed it for me. It's because *I* fixed it for me. I voiced my concerns and my desires, and the world didn't explode. I didn't need to yell in rage. And now, we're sitting here, still discussing things like friends.

Archie was right. I *did* need to do this for me.

And now, there's one more thing I need to do for myself. And for Archie. I go back to revise my to-do list.

~~*I think I might be in love with my ex-husband.*~~

I am in love with my ex-husband.

Chapter Twenty-Seven

My fist pounds on the heavy oak door, and I wait for a response. My body seems to be doing things automatically, and I'm beginning to seriously doubt my rational decision-making skills.

The casserole dish in my hand is heavy as I wait for Margaret to answer the door.

Eventually, I hear the creaking footsteps, though I'm not sure if it's the house or her joints doing the creaking.

The door opens.

"Meyer. Hello, dear. Come in. Did you come for a good sympathy cry? My friend Agnes just told me I'm horrible at those." She peers at me over her glasses. "But I did pull a batch of cinnamon rolls out of the oven just now."

"I think I prefer cinnamon rolls over a sympathy cry."

"Thank goodness. I'm much better at those."

I follow her inside and close the door after us. I set her casserole dish on the counter and glance around. Her house always seems dark with the old wood paneling inside, but it's homey. It must be the hours I've spent here, taking piano lessons from draconian Margaret.

"So, you've lost the husband a second time."

Margaret's sharp remarks used to hurt. Probably because they hit a little too close to home for my comfort. But now that I know what a softy she is underneath—I recognize them for what they are: concern.

"I lost him again," I agree as I take the plate with two cinnamon rolls from her. They smell divine.

"Is there another man?"

"No, there isn't another man!" I shoot back. "What kind of woman do you take me for?"

Margaret shrugs. "Well, there was that good-looking doctor."

"Turns out, that good-looking doctor and Archie are friends. Archie is the reason that Dr. Sharpe applied for the job here. They met in Arizona."

"Ah. It's a real shame that boy isn't interested in me. I told him I was loaded."

She scoops another cinnamon roll onto a plate while I try to swallow without choking.

"What? You think just because I'm old that I'm blind? I've been trying to break a hip for over a month so I can go visit him in the ER."

"I mean this with the utmost respect, but you frighten me."

"Good. I'm glad to know I'm not losing my edge. Care to tell me why you're really here? I've never seen you go to anyone for a mope-fest before. I've always assumed that's what your sister is for."

I clear my throat and set down the plate that's still

heavily laden with cinnamon rolls. "You're right. I came here with something specific in mind."

Margaret adjusts her glasses. "Well, what is it? I hate anticipation."

"But do you hate Arizona?"

"This is the most fun I've had in ages!" Margaret cackles as she physically drags me onto the plane. "Now, where are we sitting?"

I shakily hold up our tickets, and she glances at the seat numbers.

"You put us in the nosebleed section! You couldn't even spring for first class?"

"Back row is the safest," I whisper as the flight attendant greets us with a smile.

She won't be smiling when we're crashing through the air in a burning ball of fire.

I plant my feet.

Margaret turns to me. "Why are you doing this?"

"Because I love Archie, and he loves me," I repeat my mantra.

"Good girl. Now, let's go find our seats."

Margaret gives me a firm push forward, and I hug my bag to my chest as I stumble into a gentleman sitting in first class.

There's lots of pausing and stopping as people shove their bags into overhead bins. A small child runs down the aisle and then back to his frazzled parents.

Eventually, we make it to our seats, and I stow both of

our carry-on bags with the help of a friendly flight attendant.

I must look frightened because the nice woman looks me in the eye.

"Are you okay?"

"No. I hate flying."

"Oh, you poor thing. Why don't you sit down, and I'll be right back." She disappears into the back and returns a moment later with a water bottle and a vomit bag. She passes both to me. "Just in case. Let me know if I can help with anything else!"

"Is there any chance we can drive this plane to Phoenix?"

She laughs as if I were the funniest person alive.

Margaret smacks my leg. "Hush. You're embarrassing me. I need her to like me. I want to enjoy my flight with all the drinks and snacks I can get."

I close my eyes, but that makes the nausea and dizziness worse.

I fling open my eyes and pick something to stare at. Someone sitting in front of me has a mole on their neck. It's very interesting. I've never studied moles before, but I could. Maybe I should have been a dermatologist. I can always go back to school. It's not too late.

"Ladies and gentlemen, if you could all find your seats and stow your bags, then the flight attendant will review all safety measures, and we'll be underway in no time."

The ding of the seatbelt light shoots through my soul.

"Didn't you bring a book or anything?" Margaret asks as she studies me.

"I forgot."

"Here, have one of mine." She begins digging through her giant purse. She jerks out three books from the bottom and spreads them out to show me the titles.

"I'm not sure I can read right now."

"Reading is good for your soul. So is traveling."

"Then, I think my soul has all the good it can handle right now."

Margaret is the one who got me hooked on reading. She introduced me to my first historical-romance novel, and there was no turning back.

But right now, my brain isn't even processing the flight attendant's safety instructions. Am I supposed to put other people's air masks on first? Open the emergency hatch door? I don't know.

By the time we're in the air, I'm pretty sure I'm going to die. Not because of a plane crash, but because my body is going to simply shut down on me after I've put it through too much.

At some point in the flight, Margaret tries to pass me a book again.

There's a shirtless man on the cover, and it's startling enough to jerk me out of my intense state of fear.

"What's this?"

"We call those *books* where I come from, dear."

Margaret goes back to reading another book and sips some alcoholic beverage. I don't even remember when the flight attendant brought it for her.

"Read it. It will take your mind off of everything."

I blow a slow breath out through my lips. "I'm afraid if I do that, then I'll get nauseated again."

"Okay, I'll read out loud to you, then." She snaps the book out of my hands and proceeds to read—quite loudly, I might add—*The Viking's Lady*. Apparently, Vikings wandered around shirtless, staying warm by the overload of testosterone in their system.

Margaret ends up with a rapt audience and an impromptu book club with the passengers nearest her. Time passes blissfully for a while as all of us are absorbed in the Margaret bubble.

For a brief time, I'm blissfully unaware of what landing the plane will entail.

Chapter Twenty-Eight

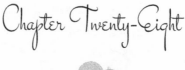

I stumble into the office building in the Phoenix business district.

Holly had been a dear and sent me the address to his workplace. I'm pretty sure my Uber driver didn't even bother coming to a complete stop as I jumped out of the car. He was ready to get the vomit smell out of his car.

I hit the button for the elevator.

"Can I help you?"

I freeze, thinking of all the things this voice could mean. They're about to throw me out. I look like a vagabond. I smell horrible, I look horrible, and I definitely don't look like I belong in a high-rise building. My bangs are sticking in forty-nine different directions, and there's a margarita stain on my left shoe. I turn around to find a security guard standing there. He's as old as my grandpa, and he has a pleasant smile on his face.

"I'm looking for my husband. I've never actually come to his work before, but this is kind of an emergency."

The man looks at me and nods slowly.

"I could tell that you were in trouble. I've got a good eye for these kinds of things. I am happy to help."

I paste something on my face, and I hope it resembles a smile.

"Where does he work?"

"JL Design."

"Oh, yes, of course. That's on floor three. Let me get this elevator going for you." He punches the button, and the elevator opens right up for him. "Now, you just head up there and give them the name of your husband, and they'll direct you right to him."

I smile and fight the urge to envelop him in a big warm hug. I smell disgusting, and I don't want him to smell it.

If I had plotted this out, I would've taken the time to go shower, rinse the airport germs and panic from my body, and then come to find Archie in a killer dress.

But I have to do this before I lose my courage. I've come to the realization that I only have small doses of courage each day.

And the quicker I get it over with, the better.

The elevator dings, and I step out slowly, careful to avoid the crack between the floor and the elevator. It opens right up into an open office.

There's no private lobby. It's a sea of desks and bustling activity. I have an overwhelming urge to hurry back to my safe and sweet security guard, but I can't seem to pry my eyes from the hype of activity in the office.

Everyone's wearing a suit or some form of formal business attire. My eyes land on the receptionist—or at least, that's who I'm assuming it is—and she seems stunned by my presence.

I take a tentative step toward her, but she recoils. Every single hair on her head is where it should be. She's probably afraid my bang situation is catching.

"Meyer?" a shocked voice rings out from somewhere in the sea of people.

I turn around, scanning for that voice, looking for the man it belongs to. I spot him standing behind a desk, a tablet in his hand, surprised look on his face, and a suit that was made for him on his body.

Dang, I'm gonna have to rethink my thoughts on casual wear if he looks like this in a suit. Black-tie events don't sound as intimidating if I get to look at that all evening.

He sets down the tablet and takes hesitant steps toward me. "Meyer, what are you doing here?"

Panicking.

"I came to pick up something that belongs with me." I take a step toward him. I stop a foot away.

"What happened to you?"

I swallow a wave of nausea and shake my head. "Trust me, you don't want to know."

"What's that smell?" someone in close vicinity to us asks.

Archie looks as though he wants to be excited, but he's not sure that he can trust what he sees.

A small smile crosses his lips. "Are you really standing in my office in Phoenix right now?"

"I sure hope so. Otherwise, I've got a real big problem."

Archie throws back his head and laughs. "But how did you get here?"

A reel plays across my mind—bombs, airplanes, vomit bags, the audio of an old World War II propaganda clip.

Archie takes in my glassy-eyed look. "You didn't fly, did you?"

I nod slowly.

"Oh no, you poor baby." He holds out his arms and steps forward to wrap me in a hug.

I hurry and plant a hand on his chest. "Trust me, you don't want to touch me right now. We landed forty minutes ago"—I gesture to my body—"and I know it's not pretty. But I had to come see you first thing."

Archie ignores my staying hand and hugs me anyway. "I don't care, Meyer. I can't believe you got on a plane. For me." He pats my head gently as he trails his fingers through my hair.

"Yes, I've been taking your advice and learning to speak up for what I want. And I want you." I wrap my arms around his waist and lock my hands together behind his back. "I wanted to show you how much I want you in my life." I lean back and look at him with frantic eyes. "I know I should've cleaned up before I came to see you, but I needed to see you right away. I need to ask you something important."

I push out of his arms and kneel on the ground. I reach into my back pocket and pull out the avocado.

"What did the avocado half say to the other avocado half?"

Archie's shaking with laughter. I find myself fighting

a grin as well. I've never been this ridiculous for anyone. And it's about time I started.

"Without you, I am empty inside."

I hand him the avocado, and he flips it over twice in his hand before he lets out a loud whoop and scoops me up into his arms. He plants a kiss on my lipstick-smeared lips and hugs me tight.

He finally sets me down, turns to the office, and says, "This is my wife!"

There's an awkward little cheer, and then Archie is carrying me toward the elevator.

He bumps the button with his elbow and smiles down at me.

I ask, "Am I going to get you in trouble with your job?"

"Technically, I'm not even supposed to be working today. I decided to come into the office because I couldn't get a pretty brunette off my mind."

"Well, who is it?" I tease.

"I'm holding her right now."

We reach the ground floor, and after a brief argument, I convince Archie to set me down and allow me to walk.

The security guard is pacing back and forth when we walk out of the elevator, hand in hand.

His face cracks into a grin. "You found him!"

"I found him! I'm going to keep him, too!"

Archie and I laugh at the slightly confused look on his face as we walk out.

"Where are your things?"

"At the hotel with Margaret," I say as I climb into his car.

Archie stops before he slams the passenger door. "Did you say *Margaret*?"

I grin sheepishly. "I wish I could say I was brave enough to fly down here by myself...but I needed help. Margaret was my willing victim. She'd been wanting to go somewhere warm for a while. She said this spring was going to be the death of her."

"What did she have to say about flying with you?" Archie rests his arms on the door and grins at me.

I tap my fingers against my knees. "Now, let me think a minute. I think it was something along the lines of, '*Never again.*' She didn't phrase it as nicely, though."

We make it to the hotel, and I can hear the TV blaring as I reach the room. I knock on the door loudly.

Margaret calls, "Come in!"

I enter the room. I want a toothbrush and a shower, that way I can relax and enjoy just *being* with Archie.

I stop short at the sight that greets me. Margaret is wearing a sunhat and a robe. "I'm heading to the pool, and there's nothing stopping me." She slides a giant pair of sunglasses on over her reading glasses. "Oh, did you find Archie?"

"Yes. He's waiting in the hall."

"Oh, good. Is he coming home?"

"I don't know, but I think we're fixing things."

She squirts a generous about of sunscreen on her

hand then slathers it on her cheeks. "So, I didn't sit through that hellish flight with you for nothing."

I shake my head with a smile. "No. It was definitely for something. And seriously, Margaret, I cannot thank you enough."

She cuts a hand through the air, a drop of sunscreen lands on the carpet. "Make sure that I get to play at your next wedding."

She marches past me and into the hall.

"Hello, sweetie," she greets Archie. "I'm on my way to go sunbathing."

Archie steps into the hotel room after Margaret leaves. "I can't believe you went traveling with Margaret. I've always wanted to travel with Margaret! She's so cool."

"I know. Everyone loved her on the plane, and she ended up with a million free drinks. How does one person become that amazing? It's frightening."

"You're frightening. And I mean that in the nicest, most loving way." He studies me from my toes to the top of my head.

"Is it the bangs?"

"No, it's the crazed look in your eye. It looks like you faced your biggest fear and barely lived to tell about it." His grin is far too big on his face, as though he's ridiculously pleased that I made such an effort for him.

"Yep. That's exactly how I feel." I pull my shirt away from my stomach and look at it. "I'm not sure what's stuck on here, but we probably don't want the answer to that."

Archie steps forward and latches a hand onto my arm, pulling me closer. "Meyer, I need to kiss you."

I hold up both hands and push out of his hold. "Give me five minutes. That's all. I just need five minutes."

I grab my backpack off the chair where I tossed it when I made sure Margaret was settled in the room before I ran off in search of Archie.

I hurry into the bathroom, locking the door as I hear Archie come closer.

"I don't care Meyer!" He calls through the door.

"I do! I'm disgusting! Five minutes Archie." I strip out of my clothes and turn the water on.

"I've been waiting a lot longer than five minutes, Meyer." His voice sounds sultry even through the heavy wooden door.

I brush my teeth while I wait for the shower water to warm up.

"Better make it fast..." He calls out again. "I'm putting on the Do-Not-Disturb sign."

I nearly choke as I hurry and rinse.

Fastest shower in the history of Meyer Dunmore's life.

I don't bother with makeup because I'm already past my time limit of five minutes, but at least I'm clean now. I won't be sharing the vomit scent and spreading nastiness all over him.

Besides, given the fact that I open the door to find him reclining on the bed with his shirt unbuttoned? He probably would knock in the door if I took any longer.

His eyes go wide when he sees me standing there wrapped in a towel.

"Best. Day. Ever."

Chapter Twenty-Nine

"Are you sure it's safe to leave Margaret in Phoenix by herself?" I ask as I turn the air-conditioning higher.

The Arizona heat is wilting my Oregon-born body. My lips are chapped, and my skin is dry. A desert flower, I am not.

We're driving back home. Together.

Archie shakes his head. "You're asking the wrong question. You should ask if it's safe for Phoenix to leave Margaret there."

I laugh at that because he's right. The woman loves to travel. And she told me that the dry desert air is making her joints feel better. She said it shaved thirty years off and that she might never come home to Oregon. But we both know we'll see her in a week's time—because we are heading home to get married. And she wouldn't miss the chance to play piano at our wedding...again. She told me that we were doubly blessed by her piano playing since she played at our first wedding. She said we were an extra-special case and that our marriage would definitely last this time. She said the first time was a practice round.

The fact that we're getting back together means that she still has a perfect record. I often wonder if that perfect record is due to the fear that Margaret would come make her people pay. Wouldn't surprise me if Margaret had some ties to the mafia or something along those lines.

The car hums along quietly. Archie told me he wouldn't make me fly again. He kept telling me how brave I was.

All I can think is, it's a good thing he didn't see me on that flight. I swore Margaret to secrecy on how bad it really was. Margaret promised me that it was an experience she did not wish to repeat with me ever, which is probably the real reason she stayed behind in Phoenix. She didn't want to risk being forced onto an airplane with me again. She told me that she'd arrange for her own flight back.

She is marvelous. And so is the man sitting next to me.

He packed up his car with as many of his personal belongings as he could fit, and now, we're road-tripping back to Oregon. We might even spend the night in Las Vegas on our way.

I reach my hand across the console and lace my fingers through his. "I missed you. I'm sorry I was such a butthead."

"I'm sorry I didn't fight for us," Archie says. "I just left."

He pulls onto the highway, and I watch the passing desert. So open. So hot. So different than Oregon.

"After I told you to go. That wasn't exactly fighting for us either."

Archie shrugs. "Yes, but I should've known. I should've listened more to what you really wanted, what you really needed in our relationship. Instead, I was pushing my own ideas of what you should be."

"And I did the same thing to you," I reply.

"Do you think we've finally matured enough to realize that we can't change the other person?"

"I'm willing to try if you are," I say. "What are we going to do in Vegas?" I ask.

I kick my shoes off and put my feet up on the dash. He reaches over and smacks them down.

"Pay attention to your driving!" I bark at him.

"Look at us, just like an old married couple. Isn't that sweet?"

"I'll give you something old and..." I mutter.

"I read an article about people getting in wrecks when their legs are on the dash. It shatters bones. Don't do that."

"Okay, Mr. Bossy Husband Pants."

"You're always so sassy to me."

"I save it all for you," I reply with a smug smile.

"And I love all of it."

Chapter 30

One week after my fateful flight to Arizona, and we are getting married.

We applied for a marriage license online somewhere between Phoenix and Vegas, and thankfully, Archie has never officially changed his residency information, so it was a painless experience to get the license.

Our local pastor was willing to marry us the minute we got home.

This time, we're doing the wedding exactly how I imagined. It's small. It's in our backyard.

Margaret is once again at the piano.

Our families are here.

Gatsby is the best man, though he seems to have completely forgotten his duties and is busy batting at the ribbon hanging from my bouquet.

"Do you, Archie Dunmore, take Meyer Dunmore to be your lawfully wedded wife?"

Someone from the peanut gallery coughs outs, "Again."

They get hushed. My bets are on Kingston as the offender.

"I do," Archie says with a grin.

"Do you, Meyer Dunmore, take Archie Dunmore to be your lawfully wedded husband?"

"Avocado. I mean, I do."

Archie grins.

"You may kiss the bride."

Archie swoops forward and bends me backward over his arm. He gives me a big kiss amid the whoops and whistles.

When we finally stand upright and Margaret begins playing the wedding recessional song, I'm a little light-headed and a lot happy.

"Did you choose this song?" Archie murmurs into my ear.

I take a moment to pay attention to what Margaret is pounding out on those keys and bark out a laugh.

She's playing "Another One Bites the Dust."

"That woman." I shake my head as Archie loops his arm around my waist and drags me behind the arbor.

"This woman," he growls, and he dips for another kiss.

When we finally come up for air, I manage to say, "Oh no! I forgot to put clean sheets on the guest bed for you!"

"Cake!" A sharp yell breaks us apart like guilty teenagers making out in the back seat of their parents' car.

Archie mutters something not nice under his breath then turns back to Margaret.

She holds a knife toward him, blade first. "There has to be cake before a honeymoon."

I hold my hand in front of my mouth as I whisper to Archie, "I think she might stab us if we don't."

"Okay fine, we'll cut the cake." He snorts. "But then we are going on that honeymoon."

I carefully take the knife from Margaret and follow her back to where a cake sits on the table.

My heart feels as though it might burst as I look around at our friends and family. A small wedding is everything I dreamed it would be.

Archie laces his fingers through mine and leads me around to the other side of the cake table. We pause as the photographer snaps a few pictures before we join hands on the knife and awkwardly cut the cake. I don't know who thought this was a good first activity for married couples, because if it's an omen for the rest of marriage, ninety nine percent of marriages are doomed. The cake slice is crooked, and we barely escape unhurt.

I lift the small piece in my hands and turn to Archie. I ask him softly, "Do you remember when you accused me of mashing cake in your face?"

"Yes," he answers immediately.

"Well, I don't want there to be any doubt in your mind this time."

"You're so good to me." Archie leans down to kiss me.

I give him a lingering kiss on the lips... right before I smash cake in his face.

The white frosting makes his skin look tan. And the shocked look in his eyes nearly makes me cackles with glee.

"I knew it!" He's nearly as gleeful as me. "I knew it wasn't an accident. Come here."

He abandons the small piece of cake in his hand and instead grabs both sides of my face and leans forward to kiss me. Sweet frosting and the scent of vanilla combine with the zap of electricity I get every time Archie kisses me.

It's hard to keep laughing when someone is kissing you, so I abandon that track and switch to the kissing Archie train.

There's nothing better, after all.

Epilogue

"Put her down!" I yelp as I run after Archie. It's been four years since we've been married. (Again.)

Four years since we recommitted to one another. I couldn't be happier. Maturity, growth, forgiveness. Those three have been good to Archie and me.

And now we get to enjoy each other every day for the rest of our lives.

We also get to enjoy every day with Bristol Grace Dunmore. Eighteen months old with her father's twinkling eyes and already my thick hair. Note to self: no bangs for Bristol until she's old enough to take on the responsibility herself.

Archie is hoisting Bristol up and down in the air like an airplane. Her loud laughter is scaring the birds out of the trees as we walk around the lake.

After adding on to our sweet little cottage in our first year of (re)marriage, we began having serious discussions about children. We both wanted kids. But we were both so happy together. It was hard to imagine adding another person to the mix.

Bristol ended that discussion with her arrival on her due date. A scary, little punctual thing. It probably had to do with all the times Willa spoke to her in the womb. Bristol had picked up on her habits already.

"You're going to scare her!" I call as I hurry to catch up.

Bristol is now flying steadily higher. She is not afraid, despite my warning.

Archie gathers her close to his chest and stage whispers, "Remember, we only fly when mom isn't looking."

I scowl at him. "We don't joke about that."

"More, more, more," Bristol chants as she jerks her whole body upward in an attempt to make Archie fly her again.

It's frightening how much she is like her father. He's kept his flight times minimal, knowing I dread it, but he's thrived in his new career as an airplane mechanic. Now that Lawrence has officially retired, Archie is head mechanic at the Green Valley airport. One of my favorite parts of his job is that we get to eat lunch together every day.

Now that Bristol is getting older it's one of her favorite parts of the day as well. She grabs her shoes and goes to stand next to the door when it's lunch time and says 'dada' on repeat until I carry her out to the car.

Today we packed a picnic lunch and ate at the lake.

"Are you trying to get me in trouble with your mom?" Archie asks Bristol as she keeps trying to 'fly.'

Bristol grabs his face and pinches his lips with her adorable chubby fingers. "Yes."

"I swear she understands everything." Archie says after he plants a kiss on her cheek.

Bristol returns the favor, leaving a string of drool hanging off the stubble that's been growing the last few days.

I never knew growing molars was such a slobbery affair, but Archie routinely shows me a soaked patch on his t-shirts after she's fallen asleep snuggled against his chest.

Archie sets Bristol down on top of his shoes and slow walks her close to me. "Show momma that you're okay."

"Mom, mom, mom!" She squeals as Archie takes fast but small steps, making her cheeks shake with laughter.

Archie stops directly in front of me and stage whispers to Bristol, "I better kiss mommy until she forgets about flying."

"Fly!" Bristol cries out then makes the motor sound as Archie leans toward me.

"I'll admit you look like you'd rather bite me than kiss me," he whispers with a grin.

"It did cross my mind..." He's not entirely wrong. I've slowly been getting better at voicing my actual opinions over the years. Rather than staying silent. Archie has been incredibly supportive of it, and often the one I practice on. I've successfully said 'no' at least ten times in four years... okay, maybe more than that, but it's a work in progress. One that I'm grateful for his support in. Which is why I do my best to not nag—too much—about the whole flying thing.

Archie leans forward and presses a kiss on my cheek. "I'm sorry pumpkin."

"Are you? How sorry?"

His eyes twinkle as he kisses the corner of my lips. "I'll make it up to you."

"I think I like the sound of that."

"Sparkling apple juice tonight? After Bristol's in bed?"

"It's a date." I lean forward and kiss him. Happy knowing that despite our still very unequal love of flying that this time we are going to work through it.

Acknowledgments

Thank you for reading Forget Me Twice! Archie and Meyer's story jumped (crashed?) at me, and I had to set aside all plans and write it. The story would not be silenced. I hope you fell in love with them as much as I did!

Thank you so much to my editors, Jovana, Jenn, and Alison, who have been patient with me and the amount of times I can repeat a word in a sentence, or forget that someone was sitting and also standing at the same time.

Thank you to Molly for giving me name inspiration! (Meyer is perfect for her.)

Thank you Sarah and Ashley for listening to me rant about this idea for an entire year as I worked on it.

Thank you to the many beta readers, ARC readers, and of course Lucy for designing such a beautiful cover.

Being a writer is NOT a lonely thing with such an amazing support system and incredible readers.

Neighbors Like That

KYLIE

He started our war—I intend to finish it. Buying a house in the suburbs was supposed to be low stress: my own little haven to decorate and landscape exactly how I want.

Instead I find myself locking my garbage can to keep pests out—pests that are six-foot-one, green-eyed, and far too good looking.

My trespassing neighbor is rude and entitled. It isn't long before war is declared and I find myself stooping to immature pranks.

When trouble lands at my door, my unlikely neighbor starts knocking on my heart. Was I ready to answer?

HAGEN

I will win no matter what it takes. I moved to this neighborhood for a fresh start. The one thing I'm not looking for is a relationship, so when I mistakenly assume my neighbor is hitting on me, I lash out at her. I didn't mean to start the war, but now she taunts me from across the street.

Our harmless pranks have become the highlight of my day. I should stay away—but I can't. I want to spend more time with her.

When a stalker begins sending Kylie a series of notes, I'm only too willing to help protect her. Maybe I'm looking for a relationship after all.

Mr. H.O.A.

A condemned apartment building means I'm stuck sleeping in my car. My carefully planned future—gone.

It's just bad business to admit to being homeless when you're the top selling real estate agent in the county. So when a fellow evictee, Nola, comes up with a solution to my homeless situation, I take her up on her offer.

An empty house with a gorgeous roommate? *Sign me up.*

I didn't know that staying at her friend's house would lead to us pretending to be married. I didn't know I would get elected to be president of an HOA I have no business being a part of.

And I'm beginning to suspect my beautiful, devious, fake wife isn't telling me everything.

What happens when we get another roommate, and our deception moves to the next level?

Nola is the whirlwind I didn't want in my life—but she just might be exactly what I need.